Daphne got back into position — and once again Prince Albert turned. "You think you're pretty funny, don't you?" she accused, though a smile played on her lips.

Taylor grinned, too, despite her worries. Prince Albert's antics would be comical — if there wasn't so much at stake.

"Get a chain shank and yank him," a girl's voice advised from behind them.

Taylor's shoulders tightened. She knew Plum Mason's voice anywhere.

"You have to show him who's boss," Plum added. "You can't just let him do what he wants."

"He's a little shy of people yet," Mrs. LeFleur told Plum.

Plum shot Mrs. LeFleur a tight smile. "Is that the horse I'm going to lease?"

Ride over to
WILDWOOD STABLES

WILDWOOD STABLES

Playing for Keeps

BY SUZANNE WEYN

SCHOLASTIC INC.

New York   Toronto   London   Auckland
Sydney   Mexico City   New Delhi   Hong Kong

ISBN: 978-0-545-14980-8

Copyright © 2010 by Suzanne Weyn
All rights reserved. Published by Scholastic Inc.
SCHOLASTIC, APPLE PAPERBACKS, and associated logos are trademarks and/or registered trademarks of Scholastic Inc.

12 11 10 9 8 7 6 5 4 3 2 1   10 11 12 13 14 15/0

Printed in the U.S.A.   40
First printing, March 2010

For *Jill and Danny Bergstresser* of
JD Performance Horses of Oswego, New York.
And with thanks to *Diana Gonzalez* for
sharing her horse expertise.

Chapter 1

Taylor Henry clicked her tongue softly and dug her knees into Prince Albert's sides. She pressed the heels of her brown cowboy boots down into the stirrups. The black quarter horse gelding immediately moved from a walk into a smooth jog, keeping to the sides of the corral. Leaning forward in the saddle, Taylor loosened the reins a bit and signaled Prince Albert to go a little faster. "Good boy," she praised as he broke into a steady lope.

It felt so great to be riding again!

How she'd missed it!

Taylor steered Prince Albert toward Daphne Chang, who sat on the top rung of the wooden split-rail corral fence, watching. At fifteen — tall and slender with long, silky black hair — Daphne was, so far, the only instructor giving lessons at the newly reopened horse ranch, Wildwood Stables.

For more than twenty years the once-thriving ranch had been abandoned, left to decay and splinter. Now, though, it was coming back. It was just about nine on a Saturday morning, and tradespeople had already arrived to continue the scraping, sanding, hammering, sawing, and painting they'd been working at for the previous two weeks. The dilapidated stable, corrals, and supply sheds were well on their way to being restored. Taylor recalled how, when she first came upon the place, it had reminded her of a ghost town. All that was missing were the tumbleweeds. Now she gazed at the many improvements and couldn't resist a quick shiver of pride. She had played such a big part in getting the place reopened that she felt as if it were a part of her.

Daphne smiled at Taylor and Prince Albert as they approached. "He rides like a dream," she commented, "when *you* ride him."

Taylor dismounted and took off her helmet, letting her long brown ponytail swing around her shoulders. She did a quick knee bend to get rid of that stiff, bowed-leg feeling she always experienced after being on a horse. Brushing dust from her jeans and red shirt, she offered Prince Albert's reins to Daphne. "Want to try him?" she asked. "He's had a couple of weeks to get to know you. Maybe he won't be so spooky anymore."

Daphne eyed Prince Albert uncertainly. "Are you going to behave for me, boy?" she asked, her voice full of skepticism.

Daphne was an expert rider who preferred English, but she could ride both English and Western style. Normally, there should have been no doubt that she'd hop on Prince Albert and handle him beautifully. But Prince Albert was not behaving normally.

Taylor stroked the side of Prince Albert's smooth, muscular neck. "Be nice to Daphne," she coaxed. "She's our friend. And it's really important that you let other people ride you."

Prince Albert neighed, but Taylor couldn't tell if it meant yes or no — or anything at all — so she pretended it was a yes. "Good, I'm glad you're going to cooperate," she praised her horse. Taylor looked to Daphne. "See? He says you should come on up."

"Oh, yeah?" Daphne questioned with light laughter as she hopped down into the corral. "We'll see about that."

Taylor wished she could make Prince Albert understand how crucial it was that he allow people other than her to ride him. It wasn't an exaggeration to say that nothing less than his life depended on it.

Prince Albert sputtered nervously and turned toward Taylor. "It's all right," Taylor assured him, nodding her head.

Facing Prince Albert, Daphne breathed into his nostrils. In the wild, horses did this to get to know one another. Horse trainers and owners used the method to let their horses become familiar with them. Daphne and Taylor had agreed to have Daphne try it. Prince Albert had to meet and trust as many people as possible.

The horse seemed to be paying attention to Daphne's breathing. Was he learning anything about her, things his keen horse sense picked up in her breath? Or was he simply memorizing her scent?

Taylor felt a flicker of jealousy as she watched Daphne try to connect with Prince Albert. She might be sharing Prince Albert with the ranch, but his heart was all hers. Taylor loved that she and Prince Albert shared a bond.

That he preferred her to anyone else was a secret source of deep happiness. It hurt a little that she would have to give up that precious exclusivity.

Taylor knew, though, that she had to squelch her instinctive possessiveness and encourage Prince Albert to befriend other humans. The gelding needed to be a school horse, one that could be used for lessons, in order to pay for his board here at Wildwood Stables. It was the arrangement Taylor had struck with Mrs. LeFleur, who had just inherited the place. If Mrs. LeFleur couldn't use Prince Albert for riding lessons, she couldn't afford to keep him there for free. And if Mrs. LeFleur wouldn't keep Prince Albert there, then Taylor couldn't keep him at all.

"Here goes nothing," Daphne remarked as she put on the helmet, adjusting the strap below her chin. Coming along Prince Albert's side, she put her foot in the stirrup and grabbed hold of the all-purpose saddle on the horse's back. At the moment she was about to pull herself up, Prince Albert took two steps sideways, away from her.

Daphne's arms windmilled as she was pitched backward.

Taylor rushed in to grab her from behind. Both of them staggered before falling backward onto the dirt.

"Albert!" Taylor scolded, using the name she'd found on his original stall before she'd changed it to Prince Albert. "That wasn't nice!"

Daphne got to her feet first and offered Taylor a hand to get up. "What are we going to do with you, Prince Albert?" she asked, laughing as she dusted off her jeans.

Daphne's laughter was infectious, and Taylor realized they must have looked pretty funny as they wheeled backward in the corral. But Taylor's smile faded when she looked up and noticed Mrs. LeFleur watching them from behind the window of the main building across the way. If she'd seen the way Prince Albert was acting, Taylor was sure that Mrs. LeFleur wouldn't see anything amusing about it.

Chapter 2

Mrs. LeFleur approached the corral leading Albert's friend Pixie, a cream-colored Shetland pony mare, behind her. Seeing Mrs. LeFleur and Pixie together made Taylor notice how alike the pony and the ranch's owner were. Both were short, compact, and just past middle age. Pixie's frizzy, unruly mane seemed like the equine version of Mrs. LeFleur's curly hair. All Pixie needed was a pair of thick glasses and she'd be the pony version of Mrs. LeFleur, Taylor thought.

"Perhaps Prince Albert would be more at ease if Pixie were nearby," Mrs. LeFleur suggested as she opened the corral gate and led the small pony inside.

"Maybe," Taylor agreed.

"Here's your pal, Prince Albert," Daphne said.

Prince Albert went to Pixie and they nuzzled noses affectionately. "They're so sweet together," Daphne noted, and Taylor nodded.

Mrs. LeFleur stroked Prince Albert's side. "How are you today, Your Highness?" she asked him. She looked to Daphne and Taylor. "He doesn't seem to mind me petting him."

"He's okay being around people, but he only wants Taylor to actually be in the saddle," Daphne said.

"Want to try riding him?" Taylor offered.

Mrs. LeFleur shook her head vehemently. "I haven't ridden in thirty years."

"You can't own a horse ranch and not ride," Daphne objected.

"Apparently I can," Mrs. LeFleur disagreed. Taylor thought she saw a distant — and sad — look come into Mrs. LeFleur's eyes. Mrs. LeFleur's thick glasses made reading her expression difficult, and Taylor couldn't be certain. But a soft wistfulness had come into her voice, and it made Taylor wonder what Mrs. LeFleur's past experience with horses had been. Why had she stopped riding thirty years ago?

"There's no need for me to ride," Mrs. LeFleur said briskly, seeming to throw off the melancholy moment. "Daphne, now that Pixie is here, see if you can ride Prince Albert."

Daphne approached the black quarter horse once more. "Want to try this again?" she asked him in a friendly voice. "And this time, no dirty tricks, okay?"

Taylor sucked in a quick breath and crossed her fingers. Mrs. LeFleur was being nice, but Taylor knew she was serious about having Prince Albert tolerate other riders. Her budget had been stretched thin from the start, and she'd told them that the renovations were costing much more than she'd estimated. Her only hope of keeping Wildwood Stables open was to start charging to board horses as well as giving lessons and trail rides as soon as possible.

Daphne lifted her leg to slip her ankle-high paddock boot into Prince Albert's stirrup, but he turned away from her.

"Prince Albert," Taylor warned in a voice she hoped was calm but firm. "You know better than that."

Daphne got back into position — and once again Prince Albert turned. Daphne huffed with frustration, putting her hands on her hips. "You think you're pretty funny, don't you?" she accused, though a smile played on her lips.

Taylor grinned, too, despite her worries. Prince Albert's antics would be comical — if there wasn't so much at stake.

"Get a chain shank and yank him," a girl's voice advised from behind them.

Taylor's shoulders tightened. She knew Plum Mason's voice from her eighth-grade class at Pheasant Valley Middle School. Turning, Taylor faced the girl. Plum's diamond stud earrings peeked out from her long blonde hair and gleamed in the sunlight. The leather soles of her expensive riding boots were propped on the lower rung of the corral fence, and her elbows were settled on the top.

"You have to show him who's boss," Plum added. "You can't just let him do what he wants. Every good rider knows that."

"He's a little shy of people yet," Mrs. LeFleur told Plum. "We don't want to force him."

Plum shot Mrs. LeFleur a tight smile. "Is that the horse I'm going to lease?"

"Oh, are you Plum Mason?" Mrs. LeFleur inquired.

Taylor's stomach clenched. Mrs. LeFleur had mentioned that Plum's mother had called to inquire about leasing a horse. Since Prince Albert and Pixie were the only animals at the ranch, the quarter horse was all Mrs. LeFleur had to offer.

"No!" Taylor blurted.

Mrs. LeFleur looked at her sharply.

"I mean . . . I'm the only one he'll let ride him, so there's no way he could be leased," Taylor explained, more for Mrs. LeFleur's benefit than for Plum's.

"Excuse us a moment, will you?" Mrs. LeFleur said to Plum. "I need to speak to Taylor a moment . . . privately."

Chapter 3

Taylor followed Mrs. LeFleur into the ranch office. "You told me you wouldn't lease Prince Albert if you could use him for lessons," Taylor reminded her the moment they were inside.

"And I can't use him for lessons," Mrs. LeFleur countered.

"He just needs a little more time," Taylor argued. "Pixie and Prince Albert have been through so much. Maybe Prince Albert only needs some more time to settle into this new home."

About three weeks earlier, Taylor had gone out with her mom's best friend, Claire Black, on a horse rescue call. Claire was an animal rehabilitator, which meant that if an animal was found hurt or sick with no one to care for it, Claire got a call either from the sheriff or the person who'd found the animal.

Taylor had gone on plenty of these rescues with Claire, but never on one involving a horse and pony. They had discovered Prince Albert and Pixie abandoned in a small stable. No one had exercised, watered, or fed them for a long time. They had been filthy and nearly starved.

Their former owners had driven off, leaving Pixie and Prince Albert behind. When the sheriff tracked them down, they had narrowly avoided a criminal animal-cruelty charge by giving the ownership papers to Claire. Claire — knowing Taylor had always wanted her own horse — gave the ownership papers to Taylor.

But there was one major obstacle right away.

Taylor's mother and father never agreed on much, which was a major factor in their recent divorce, but they were in total accord on this: They could not afford to feed and house a horse, never mind both a horse and pony. Keeping Prince Albert and Pixie was out of the question!

And then the miracle — at least it felt like a miracle to Taylor — had happened.

When the sheriff threatened to sell Pixie and Prince Albert at a horse auction, Taylor became desperate to find them a home. She had heard about the abandoned horse ranch on Wildwood Lane and came looking for it as a possible place to keep the horse and pony. It certainly wasn't a perfect plan — the place was a wreck, and she didn't know how she'd feed and groom them properly — but it was all she could come up with.

On the evening Taylor rode Prince Albert there with Pixie following behind — the loyal pony could be counted on to follow Prince Albert wherever he went — she'd met Mrs. LeFleur, who had just inherited the place.

Summoning all her powers of persuasion, Taylor had convinced Mrs. LeFleur to reopen the horse ranch and take Pixie and Prince Albert on as trail and school horses in exchange for their board. It hadn't been all that hard to persuade her. Taylor had sensed that getting the ranch running again was what Mrs. LeFleur had really wanted to do all along; she just needed another voice urging her to follow her heart.

"Why are you so opposed to letting this girl take a lease on Prince Albert?" Mrs. LeFleur questioned. "As I told you, you would still be his owner."

"I understand that," Taylor replied. She knew all about leasing a horse. At Westheimer's Western Ranch, where she had first taken lessons, they had leased horses all the time. It meant that the person who held the lease paid each month in exchange for the exclusive right to ride a certain horse whenever they chose. But that person didn't own the horse, and the horse stayed at the ranch from which it was leased.

"Plum leased two horses from the Westheimers," Taylor explained to Mrs. LeFleur. "Both of them died."

"What?" Mrs. LeFleur cried, shocked. "Was it her fault?"

"No one is sure," Taylor admitted reluctantly. "One of them had colic so bad he died of it, and the other went lame and had to be put down."

"So it was just bad luck," Mrs. LeFleur concluded.

"I heard Mrs. Westheimer tell her husband that Plum rode the horses too hard and didn't cool them down or groom them properly afterward. She fed them while they were still overheated. They refused to lease another horse to her. You heard her out there. She wanted to put a chain shank on him. I don't even know what a chain shank is, but it sounds terrible."

"A chain shank is used for a horse that is not obeying commands," Mrs. LeFleur explained. "It's a chain that goes over the horse's nose, and the owner tugs on it to get the horse's attention."

"But Prince Albert obeys commands for me. I don't know who it was, but somebody trained him well. He does everything I want him to do." The image of Plum brutally yanking Prince Albert's head down formed in Taylor's mind and made her seethe with anger.

"How long ago did those horses die?" Mrs. LeFleur asked.

"It was two years ago. We were both eleven."

"Has she leased a horse since then?"

"I don't know. She went to some other ranch after that. I heard she tried to lease at Ross River Ranch, but I don't know why she didn't. Maybe they've heard about her, too."

Mrs. LeFleur sighed and rubbed her chin thoughtfully. "I've been told that the Westheimers have old horses that they get at auction," she said. "Prince Albert is only fifteen or so, still in his prime, so he wouldn't be as much at risk as an old horse."

In Taylor's heart, she was sure Plum was to blame

for the deaths, even though she had no absolute proof. Why else wouldn't the Westheimers lease to Plum anymore?

"I think you're jumping to conclusions about Plum," Mrs. LeFleur insisted. "Could it be that you simply don't want to share Prince Albert?"

It was true that Taylor didn't want to share anything with Plum — least of all Prince Albert. Plum got whatever she wanted! Why did she have to want something that Taylor loved so much? It wasn't fair! It wasn't right!

"Oh, please, Mrs. LeFleur," Taylor pleaded. "Plum's a horrible girl, stuck-up and mean. She's been in my class since the first grade. I know how she is. She'll hurt Prince Albert."

"Taylor, dear, we both love this place and want it to succeed. That can mean making some hard choices. Obviously, you don't like Plum, but you could be less emotional about dealing with her. I'm not so sure Plum is the horse killer you believe her to be. She may have just encountered a string of bad luck."

"I'm not wrong about her, Mrs. LeFleur. Believe me."

"Think of it as strictly business."

Strictly business? Taylor wondered what that really meant. Did it mean she should forget about her feelings? If that was what Mrs. LeFleur wanted her to do, Taylor didn't think it was possible. She couldn't believe anyone was capable of that.

Taylor felt a lump forming in her throat, but she was determined not to cry. Tilting her chin up, she gazed at the ceiling. It was her tried-and-true no-crying technique. As she felt the urge to tear up sliding back down, she knew the method had worked.

Waiting a moment until she was completely calm, she finally spoke. Though still hearing an unwanted quiver in her voice, she tried to sound collected and sensible. "It wouldn't be good business if our only horse" — Taylor hesitated as her voice caught slightly, but she forced herself to finish — "died . . . if our only horse died."

Mrs. LeFleur gazed at her kindly. "You have a point," she admitted.

"Could you just give me two more weeks to work with Prince Albert? Daphne is helping me, and she's so great with horses. And we could offer pony rides on Pixie."

"We could, but it wouldn't bring in much money."

"I'll put up signs and ask around at school. Maybe someone will want to board a horse here," Taylor suggested.

"Getting a few boards would be a good start," Mrs. LeFleur agreed. "I've exhausted most of my savings. I have a little left to keep the ranch going for about a month, but if I don't have lessons booked and boarders in these stalls by then, I'll have to close it down."

A tall, slim, blonde woman appeared in the open doorway of the office. "Hello. I'm Beverly Mason. We spoke on the phone?"

Mrs. LeFleur extended her hand graciously. "Yes. Bernice LeFleur. You were interested in a horse lease for your daughter, I believe."

Taylor tightened her hands into nervous fists, waiting for what Mrs. LeFleur would say next.

Chapter 4

Taylor was glad to see Daphne still sitting on the fence watching Prince Albert and Pixie in the corral. "What happened?" Daphne asked, her delicate eyebrows knit in concern, when Taylor hopped up onto the fence railing beside her.

Glancing around, Taylor saw that Plum was sitting in her gleaming black Cadillac SUV with her mother. The next moment, they drove off toward Wildwood Lane. Taylor sighed with relief as the vehicle disappeared around the turn in the road.

"So that was the evil Plum, huh?" Daphne prompted. "I've seen her over at Ross River, but I didn't know her name."

"Did she lease a horse over there?" Taylor asked.

Daphne shook her head. "I heard the barn manager, Bob Haynes, telling Mrs. Ross that he wouldn't do it."

Taylor sat up straighter, eager to hear this news. "Why not?" she asked excitedly.

"When he tried to correct some of her riding and aftercare habits, she didn't want to hear it."

"That's Plum, all right."

"He didn't feel she should be trusted with one of their gorgeous purebred horses — or any horse for that matter."

"Would you tell that to Mrs. L.?" Taylor requested.

"Sure," Daphne agreed. "But first, you still haven't told me — what did Mrs. L. have to say to Plum's mother?"

"That Wildwood Stables wasn't officially open for business yet. She said to come back in a week."

"A week!" Daphne was incredulous. "That doesn't give us any time at all!"

"I know," Taylor agreed.

Daphne hopped off the fence and began to pace. "I need to book lessons fast, but I can't unless I have a horse to give lessons on."

Taylor nodded sadly. "It's kind of a huge problem."

Daphne suddenly faced Taylor, her eyes bright. "That's it!"

"What's it?" Taylor asked.

"This has forced me to make up my mind. I've been thinking about bringing Mandy over here. Now I've decided to definitely do it." Mandy was Daphne's gray, mostly barb mare. Daphne boarded Mandy over at the expensive Ross River Ranch.

"The price just went up over there, and it wasn't cheap to begin with," Daphne said. "If I'm going to be here giving lessons, it just makes sense that she should be close by. I'll get to ride her more often this way, and I can use her for lessons, at least until we get Prince Albert straightened out."

"That's a great idea!" Taylor cried, suddenly feeling her spirits lift. Taylor's mother was a caterer, and she had just gotten a job at Ross River Ranch. But Taylor had never been to the stables, only seen them briefly from the school bus. "What's it like there?" she asked Daphne.

"Come over and see for yourself," Daphne suggested.

"Mandy's board is paid up until the end of the month. I have to go there tomorrow and tell them I'll be moving her. We can go for a ride."

"Awesome," Taylor said. "What time?"

"How about right after school?"

"You'll have to wait for me — the middle school gets out later than the high school. But my bus goes right past there, so getting a ride won't be a problem."

"Okay, let's do it," Daphne agreed. "I'd better go in and talk to Mrs. LeFleur to double-check that it's okay to bring Mandy."

"And tell her about Plum," Taylor called after her as Daphne headed toward the main building.

Taylor had wanted to see the exclusive horse ranch for a long time. And now she would even get to ride there, something she thought would never happen. Wildwood Stables really was the best place in the world, a place where unexpected good things just kept happening.

Swiveling around to face the corral, Taylor watched Pixie contentedly grazing on patches of rough grass growing at the fence posts. Prince Albert stood calmly, still saddled for riding. Seized with an overwhelming urge to be near them, Taylor swung her legs around and dropped into the corral.

"Hey, guys, are you up for a trail ride?" Taylor asked as she approached Pixie and Prince Albert. She tightened the girth of Prince Albert's saddle and readjusted the stirrups to fit her legs. It wasn't necessary to even harness Pixie; wherever Prince Albert went, his loyal friend would always follow.

Taylor had mounted and was walking Prince Albert to the gate when Daphne and Mrs. LeFleur came out of the main building. "Where are you going?" Mrs. LeFleur asked from the other side of the fence.

"I want to explore the trails behind the corral," Taylor replied.

"Is it safe for you to go alone?" Mrs. LeFleur questioned.

Before Taylor could reply, Daphne took out her cell phone. "What's your number?" When Taylor told her, Daphne quickly phoned it. "There, now you have my cell number and I have yours. If you don't call me in a half hour, I'm coming out looking for you."

What will you ride? Taylor wanted to ask, but she

decided not to. There was no sense bringing up the point when Daphne was just trying to help her.

"I'll take your bike, if I have to," Daphne said, seeming to read Taylor's mind.

Mrs. LeFleur's expression remained fretful, but she sighed and nodded. "I suppose the cell phones make it all right," she said. "I always forget that everyone can be contacted all the time these days."

"I won't forget to call," Taylor said with a wave as Daphne opened the gate for her.

With the pony following them, Taylor walked the horse onto a dirt trail at the back of the stable. Off to the right, pale blue mountains rose in the distance. Directly behind them, the dusty path went straight into the thick woods.

They passed an empty paddock with a broken section of fence. "Maybe someday you'll both have lots of friends here at the ranch. We'll have to fix that fence because we need the space for them all." Taylor imagined the ranch full of activity: lessons being given, trail rides going in and out, veterinarians, farriers, all sorts of people coming and going.

As they entered the woods, Taylor kept their pace to a

walk to let Prince Albert and Pixie warm up. She felt a chill as soon as they were hidden from most of the sunlight. In about a half mile she broke into a jog, and a half mile later let loose into a lope.

To be on Prince Albert out here in nature, without anyone else around — it was so perfect it felt like a dream. Being here like this was more pure happiness than she'd ever imagined she'd have, especially a few months back when she'd had to stop her riding lessons at Westheimer's because of money problems at home. Her parents' divorce had meant a tighter budget. Out here, though, she felt free and so happy.

Taylor turned back to check on Pixie. The small pony was puffing hard, struggling to keep up, her short legs moving in double time.

When she turned forward again, a low hanging pine branch hit Taylor in the face, and she started sliding off to the right. Tightening the muscles in her abdomen and legs, Taylor righted into the saddle once more. She gently pulled to a halt for a moment to calm her startled nerves and also to allow Pixie to catch up.

As she sat atop Prince Albert, Taylor listened to the thick silence of the woods. Within minutes, sounds emerged: birds calling to one another, the gurgling of a creek, snapping twigs caused by racing squirrels.

Pixie neighed as she joined them. "I know. It's so beautiful," Taylor responded as the coolness and tranquility flooded her senses.

Taylor stayed there listening to the natural sounds until she was sure Pixie and Prince Albert were sufficiently cooled down. Flicking the reins once more, Taylor guided them toward the sound of moving water. In minutes she came to a slight incline leading to a shallow creek where the water danced along, surging from one flat-topped rock to another.

Stopping by the side of the creek, Taylor dismounted. She took off Prince Albert's bridle so he could drink more easily. "Go, drink," she told them.

As Taylor watched Pixie and Prince Albert at the water's edge, noses dipped in the sparkling stream, she realized that her socks were soggy. Looking down, she groaned. The bottom of her well-worn right cowboy boot had separated from the upper part and was sunk in the mud at her feet. Checking the left boot, she saw that it, too, was starting to come apart.

Why did this have to happen? And especially when she'd been feeling as if all her cares had been left behind, at least for the moment. Now she'd have to ask her mother for new boots, which cost a lot. Taylor did not welcome the thought of having *that* conversation.

Chapter 5

That evening, Taylor sat at the kitchen table in the small farmhouse-style home she shared with her mother, Jennifer Henry. "Mom, the sole split on my brown cowboy boots. Can we go to the mall?"

Taylor's mom stood at the kitchen counter. Her blonde curls were clipped up behind her head as she fussed with one of the beaters in her handheld mixer. "Why won't this thing go in?" she muttered.

"Mom!" Taylor cried.

Jennifer looked up at Taylor, perplexed. "I'm sorry — what?"

"Spaceships have landed in the backyard, and they

want me to go back to their home planet with them. So I just wanted to say good-bye," Taylor told her.

Jennifer stared blankly for a moment, and then one side of her mouth curled into an ironic grin. "Ha-ha! Very funny," she said. "I'm sorry. I'm preoccupied by this luncheon at Mrs. Ross's next Saturday. It's a huge deal and I'm not nearly ready. Okay, so tell me again: What happened? I heard something about boots."

"My boots are no good anymore. I can't possibly wear them to Ross River Ranch. They probably won't even let me in — I'll look like a clown with my socks sticking out of the toes."

"Why are you going over to Ross River Ranch?" Jennifer asked, looking confused again.

Taylor explained how Daphne had invited her to ride. "I only want to look like I fit in," Taylor said. "I'm not even asking for riding boots, just decent heeled shoes that I can ride in — though boots would be nice."

"Okay, I suppose I can probably afford new shoes," Jennifer said, giving in.

"Thank you so much!" Taylor said, getting out of her chair to give her mother a grateful hug. "Can we go to PetFeed?"

"Why not a shoe store?"

Taylor grinned sheepishly. "Because they have an equestrian section at PetFeed," she admitted.

"And you really want the riding boots," her mom surmised.

"If I could," Taylor agreed, putting on her most adorable big-eyed puppy-dog-pleading face.

"Okay. I can't buy the most expensive boots they have, though. You understand that, right?"

"Definitely!" Taylor assured her. "You're the best — the best of the best!"

"I'm always the best when I'm spending money," Jennifer quipped.

"No, no, no! That's not true. You're always the best!" Taylor made a mental note to tell her mother how much she appreciated her at times when she wasn't asking for something.

"Do you have homework?"

Taylor nodded. "I guess I should get started."

"I guess so," her mother said with a touch of sarcasm.

"I'm going," Taylor said, sliding off her chair.

"You know our deal about keeping Albert."

"Prince Albert," Taylor corrected.

"Whatever," Jennifer said. "If your grades don't stay in the eighty to one hundred range, you will not be spending so much time down at the ranch."

"I get it, Mom," Taylor said just a little impatiently. "You've only told me a gazillion times."

"Then go!" Jennifer exclaimed, raising her voice forcefully. "Get your homework done."

Despite Taylor's casually annoyed tone, alarms were going off in her head. She'd missed a few homework assignments, and her last quiz grades hadn't been so wonderful. She'd promised herself that she'd make it all up, but so far she hadn't found the time.

Taylor scrambled out of the kitchen, snapping up her school pack from the sofa as she went. At the top of the stairs, she realized her backpack was buzzing. Fishing through it, she pulled out her cell phone and found a text message alert. Clicking onto it, she read the text from her best pal since third grade, Travis Ryan.

GO ONLINE!

Taylor's throat went dry. For some reason this text worried her. Travis sounded serious.

Taylor hurried to the computer and logged on.

She sent an instant message to Travis: WUZ UP? RU HOME?

NO. @ FRNDS. GO 2 EMAIL, he responded. SENT U VIDEO FROM PLUM'S WEB PG.

What friend? Taylor wondered. And how had he gotten onto Plum's webpage? Plum would never have accepted him as a friend if he tried to get on.

Taylor was dying to call Travis, but she didn't want to disturb him at his mysterious "friend's" house. So she logged into her e-mail account and found the message from Travis. Clicking on the video link, she was on the edge of her seat waiting for the black box that formed on the screen to reveal the video.

The moment it came on, Taylor clapped her hand over her gaping mouth.

The video's title was: THE NEW HORSE IN MY LIFE.

It showed Prince Albert grazing in the corral at Wildwood Stables.

Chapter 6

Taylor sat on the school bus with Travis the next morning. "I know you told me, but I still don't understand how you got hold of that video. Plum would never let you onto her webpage."

Travis rubbed his hand along the top of his white-blond crew cut. He puffed his cheeks in exasperation, which made his wide face look even rounder. "I told you already. One of Plum's friends sent the video to Plum's ex-boyfriend, Jake. He wrote some nasty comments about it and sent it to some of his friends. I'm friends with one of those guys, and I sent it to you."

"I can't believe she's so sure of herself. Prince Albert is my horse, you know. I have the papers."

"At least she's not buying him," Travis pointed out.

Taylor covered her face with her hands as if to block out the idea. "Don't say that! I would never sell him to her."

"What if you had to?" Travis asked.

Taylor's head swung around to stare at him with an expression of horror. "Why would I ever have to?" she demanded.

Travis opened his mouth to speak and then shut it again. But Taylor stared into his deep blue eyes and felt that she could read her friend's thoughts. She might have to sell Prince Albert if he couldn't be trained to take a rider and Mrs. LeFleur couldn't use him. If Plum was the only one who wanted him, she might have to turn him over.

Taylor folded her arms stubbornly and turned away so she was staring out the window. "Prince Albert would never let Plum ride him," she muttered stubbornly.

"I guess she's not worried about that," Travis remarked, "or she wouldn't have put that video online."

"By the way, what friend sent you that video?" Taylor asked, turning back toward him. Travis didn't have a ton of friends other than her.

"George Santos. I was at his house yesterday, and he showed it to me."

"I didn't know you were such good friends with George Santos. Since when?"

"Since you spend all your time at Wildwood Stables now," Travis said sullenly. He pulled a Wolverine comic from his pack and opened it.

"Travis! You know I've had a lot going on. Anyway, now you're going to spend all your time there, too." Taylor had convinced Travis to help with the repairs of Wildwood Stables, and when he'd come down with a box of tools, Mrs. LeFleur had appointed him Junior Head of Buildings and Grounds. Mrs. LeFleur was the Senior Head.

"Mrs. LeFleur has all those people working there. She doesn't need me," Travis grumbled.

"Yes, she does. Those workers are only there one more week, and there are tons of things still to be fixed."

"I don't even like horses," Travis insisted.

"You do so. You just haven't discovered the horse-loving part of yourself yet."

"I haven't discovered it because it's not there."

*   *   *

By the time Taylor arrived at Pheasant Valley Middle School, she had pushed the Plum problem out of her mind. The night before, fueled by her furious indignation over the video posting, Taylor had made and printed up flyers advertising Daphne's riding lessons. She figured that mentioning Daphne Chang was a plus, since Daphne was popular and well liked. Two years earlier she'd been student body president.

After dropping her books in her locker, Taylor grabbed a thick stack of the folded flyers and began stuffing them into locker vents or handing them to students who were still putting their books away.

Taylor was about to come upon Jake Richards, a tall, athletic guy who was generally considered the best-looking boy in the eighth grade. Jake was Plum Mason's ex-boyfriend. With a sudden loss of nerve, she crossed the hallway, trying to seem as if this move had nothing at all to do with him.

"Don't I get one of those?" Jake called, pivoting toward her. "How come you skipped me?"

A wave of cold anxiety shivered down Taylor's spine.

The last time she could remember Jake speaking directly to her they had both been in the fourth grade.

"I didn't think you were the horseback riding type," Taylor said. It wasn't the full reason she'd passed him by, but it was also true.

Jake laughed as he eased a flyer from the top of her stack. "Not exactly," he agreed, scanning the flyer with dancing eyes as though it were somehow amusing. "Is that old dump really open again?"

"Have you ever seen it?" Taylor asked, surprised that he knew about the place.

"Yeah, my pals and I come through the woods and ride our quads through there. It's, like, haunted or something. Have you seen any ghost cowboys rattling around?"

"It looks really good now. It's all painted and stuff. You should come take a lesson," Taylor suggested. "You definitely can't ride your quads through there anymore."

As Taylor spoke, she looked up at Jake Richards and decided he really was the best-looking guy in their grade. Most of the girls in the eighth grade towered over most of the boys, but Jake was tall. Taylor might even have fallen for him if she didn't know that half of her grade was already madly crushing on him. Besides, it would have been hopeless. Jake only paid attention to the popular girls like Plum.

"I wouldn't mind taking a lesson from Daphne Chang. She's a cutie," Jake said.

Taylor remembered the other reason she squelched any urge to get mushy around Jake. She didn't particularly like his personality.

"Daphne is in high school," Taylor remarked.

"So?" he said, not at all fazed. "Are there even any other horses there besides that old one Plum's buying? What's his name, Alfie?"

"Albert," Taylor corrected, not even bothering to conceal the annoyance in her tone. "Prince Albert, to be exact."

"You're joking, right?" Jake scoffed. "Plum made a video, and I could see that old thing's ribs."

"He is not a thing. Prince Albert is a very fine, well-trained quarter horse. He's just been neglected," Taylor said. She knew her indignation sounded prissy and maybe even a little silly, but she couldn't help herself.

"Well, once Plum buys him he can kiss his fine, well-trained quarter of a rump good-bye. All Plum's horses die. She rides them to death."

Taylor felt angry, but he was only saying what she knew to be true. So she did her best to speak calmly. "Prince Albert is not for sale, or lease. Besides, he only lets *me* ride him, so Plum won't be getting her hands on him."

Something between a smile and a sneer crossed Jake's face. "Don't be so sure. What Plum wants, she gets. Her mother always sees to that."

Chapter 7

The afternoon school bus wound its way down the steep, curving road that ran all along the east side of Ross River Ranch. Trees hid most of the fields, trails, corrals, and stable buildings, but here and there a fenced field was visible. Taylor turned toward the bus window to admire two brown geldings and a mare that grazed beside her frisky baby. "Maybe you'll get to ride one of them," Travis remarked from his seat beside her.

Taylor drew a deep, shaky breath.

"Why are you so nervous?" Travis asked. As he spoke he glanced down at her jiggling right leg.

Taylor placed her hand on her knee to settle it. "I don't

know," she admitted. "I guess I never thought I'd get to ride at such a fancy place."

"A horse is a horse, isn't it?" Travis said. "Do you think these horses neigh with classy British accents or something?"

"In a way, yeah," Taylor confessed with a self-conscious laugh. "Sort of. I bet there are only purebred horses here."

"So, what are you scared of — that you're going to crash one of them into a fence and have to pay for it?"

"NO! Of course not! Don't be dumb."

"Then what's the prob?"

"I don't know. Don't bug me about it. I'm not nervous anymore, okay?"

"Oh, no?" Travis stared pointedly at her right foot, which had started jumping without Taylor even noticing.

Taylor stopped the bounce. "No!"

A woman on horseback emerged from one of the trails, and the bus driver stopped to let her cross to the other side. Taylor looked at her from the window and immediately began hitting Travis's arm in excitement. "That's Devon Ross! It's her! She owns the ranch!"

Travis leaned over Taylor for a look at the woman. She was thin though broad shouldered, in her late fifties or early sixties, and dressed in English riding gear — jacket, breeches, high riding boots, and a velvet-covered helmet. The bay Thoroughbred gelding she rode gleamed in the afternoon sun. Its mane and tail were intricately braided.

"What a horse!" Taylor exclaimed quietly. "And she rides it so perfectly. I heard she rides dressage, or at least she used to."

"I know. You told me. It's where the horses dance ballet on tiptoe or something."

Taylor gave him a playful shove. She knew he was only teasing. He might think dressage was funny, but she admired the horsemanship skills it took to execute the complex dressage moves she'd seen on TV. She could hardly believe what she was seeing when she watched a horse rear straight up and turn with its rider in the saddle.

As the bus once again moved forward, Travis and Taylor leaned back in their seats, no longer straining to see out the window. "Do you want to come over and play Rock Band later?" Travis asked. Next to comics, playing video games was Travis's favorite pastime.

47

Taylor loved playing the drums in Rock Band. "Okay," she agreed instantly. "Is six a good time?"

"Sure."

Taylor smiled, happy they would be doing something together. She'd have to be more careful in the future to not make Travis feel so ignored.

The bus stopped at the bottom of the hill, right at the sign adorned with a drawing of a horse head and the words ROSS RIVER RANCH. Two sixth-graders got off, and with a wave to Travis, Taylor followed them out. "See ya at six," he called, waving back.

The other departing students walked off together down the road, leaving Taylor to gaze at the sign. Slinging her school pack over her shoulder, she headed down the paved tree-lined road leading to the ranch. Several shiny, sleek cars — not pickups, dusty compacts, or dented vans like the ones usually on the roads of Pheasant Valley — glided by with barely a hum.

Ross River Ranch's four closest corrals were easily three times the size of the fenced enclosures at Wildwood. Beyond the corrals were fields as far as she could see where she counted more than fifteen horses grazing. And she knew there were other fields higher up the hill. There was a large enclosed stable near the corrals and then another, much larger one, set farther back. The stable was almost as big as all of Pheasant Valley Middle School.

Taylor smiled and waved when she noticed Daphne riding toward her across the closest corral on a smallish gray mare with a thick jet-black mane and a low-set ebony tail. As Daphne got closer, Taylor saw that the sturdy-looking little horse was lightly speckled with black spots and unusual, upwardly curved ears. She recognized the ears as being similar to those of the Arabian breed of horses, since Arabians were her own favorite breed.

Taylor stepped onto the lower rung of the fence and waited for Daphne. She was relieved to see that Daphne was dressed somewhat casually in black half chaps, a hooded sweatshirt, ankle-high paddock boots, and an olive green, slightly brimmed, hunt-cap-style helmet.

"Is this Mandy?" Taylor asked when Daphne pulled up alongside the fence.

"This is my little girl," Daphne confirmed fondly. "She's the love of my life."

"She's gorgeous," Taylor said, reaching forward to stroke the side of the young mare's neck. "She has curved ears like an Arabian."

Daphne nodded. "Arabians and barbs are sort of cousins. They're both originally from North Africa, but barbs were imported to England way back in the thirteen hundreds."

"I don't see any quarter horse in her," Taylor observed, recalling that Daphne had told her there was some of Prince Albert's sensible breed in Mandy's bloodline.

Daphne tapped her helmet. "You see it up here," she replied. "Barbs are like Arabians. They're very lively and playful, but they can also be high-strung, even skittish. Mandy's pretty down-to-earth, and I think that's the quarter horse in her." Daphne twisted around and pointed to the field. "There's the most beautiful Arabian up in that field, and she's mostly sweet but she has a really nuts side, too. We can ride up there and see her later."

"Does it cost anything to ride?" Taylor asked. "I only have twenty dollars." It was the last of her birthday money from the spring. Because her mother had just bought her a new pair of brown, cowboy-style riding boots — the least expensive ones at PetFeed — Taylor couldn't bear to ask her for more money.

Daphne smiled. "Well, it would cost more than that, but don't worry. The barn manager, Bob, owes me a favor, so he said you could ride for free. Come on, we'll get you saddled up."

Daphne dismounted and walked Mandy toward the corral gate while Taylor followed on the other side of the fence. Daphne hitched Mandy to a post and then beckoned for Taylor to follow her toward the stable several yards away.

"Wow!" Taylor breathed as they stepped into the building.

Chapter 8

The stable's ceiling reached three stories, with bright sunlight beaming in from high-set windows. The horse enclosures each housed two or more horses, but they were easily four times larger than the stalls at Wildwood. Taylor could barely detect the smell of horses but inhaled the fresh scent of new hay.

"This place is amazing," she said to Daphne. "Are you sure you want to take Mandy out of here?"

Daphne's eyes darted around as though seeing the place anew through Taylor's eyes. "It is pretty great, isn't it? And no, I'm not really sure. But Wildwood Stables has so much heart, and I want it to succeed so much. Boarding Mandy there will help."

Taylor realized it hadn't really been smart to suggest to Daphne that she might not want to move her horse from this palace of a stable. Having Mandy board at Wildwood solved her problem, or at least bought her some more time to find a solution. "You're right, this place is cold and impersonal," she joked, smiling. "Who would want their horse here?"

"I know, this place is totally the pits," Daphne deadpanned. She led Taylor to a stall housing a white gelding with black spots and a black-and-white mane and tail.

"I never saw a horse like him," Taylor remarked.

"Isn't he unusual looking?" said Daphne, opening the half door and letting them into the stall. "His name is Cody and he's a Colorado Ranger."

Taylor chuckled at the funny name. "What is he, some kind of horse sheriff?"

"No. This breed was started by mixing barb and Arabian blood into a line of Virginia trotting horses. I guess the Colorado part comes in because they were used out west as ranch and cow workers. That's why I thought he'd be good for you. I know you like Western-style riding."

"It's the only kind I've learned," Taylor said.

"The other reason it would be good if you rode him is that Mrs. Ross bought him for her daughter, but she's grown and moved away. Poor Cody doesn't get ridden nearly enough," Daphne added. She patted his side affectionately. "He's got a really nice temper, don't you, boy?"

"I'd love to ride him," Taylor said as she moved in front of Cody, letting him see and get used to her a little before she hopped on. "Where do we tack up?"

"I'll show you," Daphne said. She led the way to a spacious and neat tack room. "There are no Western saddles here, but there are some nice all-purpose ones," Daphne said. Taylor noticed an array of gorgeous saddles sitting on rails along the wall.

"That's fine. I never use the saddle horn, anyway," Taylor said, referring to the knob at the front of a Western saddle that was originally intended to hold a cowboy's rope but also allowed a less experienced rider to hold on.

Daphne helped Taylor select the proper girth and stirrups. "You can use a basic bridle and snaffle bit with Cody," Daphne advised. "He's so good he doesn't need anything out of the ordinary."

They led Cody out of the stable, and with Daphne's help Taylor soon had Cody tacked up and ready to ride. "Want to ride up to the big boarding stable and see the indoor ring there?" Daphne asked.

"Sure," Taylor agreed, and swung herself into the saddle. "Let's go."

They rode toward the expansive fenced-in field below the big stable on the hill. Taylor was impressed with the fluid ease with which Daphne, without getting off her horse, was able to open the gate and then close it again once they were both in. They rode at a medium pace diagonally across the field in the direction of the stable. Taylor would have used the Western term to describe their pace and said they were jogging. She knew that the English equivalent would be the word *trot*.

Ahead of them, two groups of horses grazed peacefully. Taylor was admiring the horses closer to the stable on her left when she became aware of something moving on her right.

A chestnut horse with a white blaze was charging toward them, galloping at full speed. Taylor saw all four legs come off the ground, and the animal seemed to float in the air for a moment.

Frightened by the charging horse, Taylor pulled back on Cody's reigns. "Whoa!"

The brown horse ran a circle around the two riders, stopped, and then reared.

"What's it want?" Taylor asked Daphne in a nervous voice.

"To play."

"What? Are you kidding?" Taylor asked.

"No, I'm serious. Arabians are really playful, and when she saw us she figured we were fresh playmates. She's probably worn the other horses out. This is Shafir, the crazy Arabian I was telling you about before."

As her frightened heartbeat subsided to its normal rhythm, Taylor looked over the gorgeous deep-brown creature. The young mare had the same delicate, curved ears as Daphne's barb, Mandy, but her brown tail was high and brushlike. Taylor knew the distinctive tail was characteristic of Arabians. "Who owns her?" Taylor asked.

"I guess Mrs. Ross does, now," Daphne replied.

"What do you mean, *now*?" Taylor asked.

"She was being boarded here. The owner stopped coming or paying for her board. One day her ownership papers came in the mail."

"At least she wasn't abandoned and locked up in a shed without food or water," Taylor commented, thinking of what had happened to Prince Albert and Pixie.

The Arabian was prancing back and forth in front of them. Taylor was glad Daphne and she were on such reliable horses that wouldn't be spooked by Shafir's antics. "Could her rider handle her?" Taylor asked.

Daphne shook her head. "I think that was part of the problem. She came down and tried to work with her a few times, but I don't think she really knew what she was doing. I'd like to give it a try, but she's not my horse and I don't have the money to buy her."

"Is Mrs. Ross selling her?"

"She'd like to sell her," Daphne answered. "She already has all the school horses she needs for lessons."

"Then she might let her go pretty cheap," Taylor guessed.

"Maybe," Daphne agreed. "What are you thinking?"

"Wildwood Stables needs horses, but Mrs. LeFleur doesn't have a lot of money for them. Mrs. Ross has a horse she doesn't want . . . a horse that she's boarding for free and that she can't use — a horse you could train."

"Hmm. Shafir is really nutty, but she's friendly, too. Let's try playing with her."

"How do horses play?" Taylor asked.

Daphne pulled a red bandanna from the pocket of her hoodie. Reaching over, she tucked it into one of the cheek pieces on Cody's bridle. "Mandy and Cody like this game. Maybe Shafir will join in. It's called halters — it's like tag. Canter around a little."

Taylor translated the English riding term to mean a gentle lope. With a click and squeeze to his side, she signaled Cody to go. In a minute, Daphne and Mandy were racing up alongside them.

Mandy came closer to Cody until her mouth was nearly touching his cheek. For a frightening moment, Taylor thought Mandy was about to nip Cody. Then she saw that Daphne had pulled the bandanna from Cody's bridle. Daphne reached forward and stuffed the red kerchief into the side of Mandy's bridle. "Your turn to catch us. You're it," Daphne called.

"I'm not a good enough rider to do that," Taylor protested.

"Sure you are. Cody's done this before. We'll just trot for the first time."

"I don't know," Taylor said hesitantly.

Daphne and Mandy began moving. "Come on! You have to catch us! Don't be a wimp!"

"A wimp!" Taylor cried indignantly. If there was one thing she had never been, it was wimpy. "I'll show you who's a wimp!" she shouted as she leaned forward in the saddle and squeezed Cody's sides hard. "Giddyap, Cody! Let's get that rag!"

Daphne had been right. Cody knew just what this game was about and blasted off after Mandy. Daphne shifted Mandy into high gear and ran off, with Cody giving chase.

Taylor forgot her fear as she got caught up in the challenge of trying to cut off Mandy and Daphne. She had Cody cut a sharp right, then steered him to the left. After minutes of dodging back and forth, Cody ran neck and neck with Mandy.

New fear gripped Taylor. The two horses were so close! Would her leg be smashed between them? Stretching out a tentative hand, Taylor leaned forward and neatly plucked the bandanna from Mandy's cheek piece.

Taylor's heart was pounding, but she was grinning from ear to ear.

Daphne rode around and took it from her. "Good job!" she praised, smiling broadly. "And you thought you couldn't do it!"

"I didn't. Cody did."

"No way," Daphne disagreed. "You moved him beautifully."

"Thanks."

They both turned to see Shafir sidestepping back and forth excitedly, ears fully forward with acute interest.

Daphne rode alongside Cody and tucked the bandanna into his bridle. "Shafir wants to play so badly, but she's not sure if she's welcome. We'll go closer to her this time, okay?"

With a nod, Taylor directed Cody to jog over toward Shafir. The Arabian whinnied excitedly.

Mandy and Daphne came out after Cody and Taylor once again. Taylor gently kicked Cody to move, and the race was on. Mandy was almost close enough to grab the bandanna, but Taylor turned Cody away in time. The maneuver gave them a lead of about a foot. Taylor saw Daphne and Mandy approaching again and turned once more. This time she was aware of a chestnut brown form swooping in on her.

Shafir ran with them, not sure how to play but clearly caught up in the fun. She ran an exultant circle around them, culminating in a low, two-legged buck of joy.

"Look at her!" Taylor said admiringly to Daphne. "She's so great. We have to get her for Wildwood somehow."

Chapter 9

$\mathcal{I}$t's a nice idea, Taylor, but I'd rather not deal with that Mrs. Ross," said Mrs. LeFleur later that afternoon, when Taylor suggested that she buy Shafir. They were in the front office, the only part of the ranch that hadn't undergone any renovation.

After viewing the impressive indoor corral, Taylor had waited in front of Ross River Ranch and got on the late school bus that took kids home from afternoon activities. She wasn't really supposed to use the late bus for public transportation, but the driver was lenient about the rule.

"I know that Mrs. Ross tried to buy this place and you had to fight her in court and all," Taylor began. At the beginning of the month, Wildwood Stables had gone up for public auction due to unpaid back taxes. Mrs. LeFleur had learned of her inheritance of the ranch only after Mrs. Ross had already offered a bid on the broken-down place at auction. Mrs. LeFleur had had to fight Mrs. Ross in court to get the property back.

"But," Taylor went on, "didn't you meet Mrs. Ross when you were in court?" Taylor asked.

"No, just her arrogant, fancy lawyers."

"What if you had your lawyer speak to her lawyer?" Taylor suggested.

"I don't have the funds to engage a lawyer. I've poured every penny I have into restoring this place. You know that."

Folding her arms, Taylor leaned against the wide desk, pressing her lips together pensively. "What if Daphne and I talk to Mrs. Ross?" she suggested after some thought. In this scenario, Taylor pictured Daphne doing all the talking. The idea of actually speaking to Mrs. Ross was pretty scary.

"I don't think it's that easy to get in to see her," Mrs. LeFleur remarked.

"See who?" asked a tall, thin girl with long, thick dark brown hair. Mercedes Gonzalez was an eighth-grader at Pheasant Valley High, a recent transplant from Weston,

Connecticut. Mrs. LeFleur had recruited her to volunteer as Assistant Junior Barn Manager since she was an experienced rider and lived close to the ranch.

"Hey, I could use some help," Mercedes said when she noticed Taylor. "You're supposed to be my assistant. Remember?"

"Oh, hi, Mercedes. I'm fine. Thanks for asking," Taylor answered. She wasn't really offended. Taylor had first met Mercedes when the ranch opened, and she'd been put off by Mercedes's bossiness, but she'd since learned that Mercedes wasn't so bad under her brusque demeanor. Sometimes her manner of treating Taylor like a little kid, even though she was only a year older and in the same grade at school, was a bit hard to take. Just the same, Mercedes knew everything about horses, and Taylor knew she could learn a lot from her.

"Well, I've been here alone all afternoon," Mercedes complained. "And Pixie and Prince Albert need to have their stalls mucked, and —"

Taylor pushed herself away from the desk. "I'm coming! I'm on it! Chill!"

Mrs. LeFleur bit down on a small smile as Taylor followed Mercedes out the door. "I can see you two are developing a beautiful working relationship," she commented drolly.

Taylor stepped back into the office just long enough to roll her eyes in exasperation. "Today isn't my regular day to be here," she reminded Mrs. LeFleur to make sure she knew Taylor wasn't neglecting her responsibilities. Part of the deal Taylor had struck with Mrs. LeFleur was that she would work at Wildwood Stables three days a week in exchange for Pixie and Prince Albert's board. It was important to her that Mrs. LeFleur realize that she was holding up her end of the bargain.

"I know you're working hard," Mrs. LeFleur assured her.

"You'll think about Shafir?" Taylor pressed.

"Maybe. I don't know."

"She's a beautiful horse, and I bet you could pick her up cheap," Taylor coaxed.

"I thought you were coming to help me!" Mercedes shouted from inside a stall.

"You'd better go," Mrs. LeFleur said, scooting Taylor along with a wave of her hands.

Taylor hurried down the wide central corridor with its three inside-facing box stalls on either side. At the end on the right, she came to Pixie and Prince Albert, who stood in side-by-side stalls.

The pony neighed in greeting, while Prince Albert swiveled his ears forward alertly.

"Hiya, you guys," Taylor greeted them warmly. "How was your day today?" Taylor ruffled Pixie's frizzy forelock and then went to Prince Albert to stroke his soft muzzle.

Prince Albert snorted and then whinnied, nodding his head up and down. Taylor had seen him do this whenever she had apples. "No apples today, boy," she said apologetically. "Sorry."

Mercedes set down the buckets. "I think that Prince Albert is probably just glad to see you."

"I'm glad to see him, too," Taylor replied. "But I really think he's looking for apples. He probably smells them on me. We gave some to the horses over at Ross River." The moment she said the words, Taylor felt guilty. "I guess I should have saved two for Pixie and Prince Albert. I wasn't thinking."

Mercedes nodded down at her buckets. "Maybe he'll forget about it if you feed him. I measured out the right amount of food for each of them. I had to estimate their weight since we don't have a scale."

"Is that enough?" Taylor questioned, looking down at the bucket of feed.

"They didn't do anything but graze all day. Once they start giving lessons and trail rides, we can up the amount," Mercedes replied. She yawned and stretched. "I'm going to sweep out the tack room and straighten up in there before my mother gets here to pick me up."

"Would she mind giving me a lift home?" Taylor asked.

"No, but hurry up. She doesn't like to wait." Mercedes glanced at the buckets of feed. "You should give them fresh water now, so they can be drinking while you clean the stalls, and then feed them," Mercedes added as she headed toward the tack room at the front of the stable.

Wildwood Stables was nearly a hundred years old, so Mrs. LeFleur had needed to hire plumbers to restore the old hand pump at the back of the building. Taylor went out with a large pail and pumped the fresh, cold water that ran in underground streams below the ranch. It was getting dark, and the last birds of the day flitted from branch to branch. A half-moon had already risen but was still low in the sky.

As Taylor worked the pump handle, she felt it could

be a hundred years ago, when some other girl, a girl very much like Taylor, might have stood in the same spot and done the same thing. In her mind's eye she pictured the place as it once might have been, not so very different from the way it looked now.

This sense of timelessness — that Wildwood was a world all its own, separate from everything else — was a quality Taylor cherished. It was one of the many reasons she thought of it as the very best place in the world.

Water splashed onto Taylor's new riding boots as the pail overflowed. Realizing she'd been daydreaming, Taylor hurried back into the stable and gave Pixie and Prince Albert fresh water. Then she moved Prince Albert into an empty enclosure while she picked out his stall with a metal rake, removing the day's droppings. She worked all the straw bedding into one corner, removing more soiled bedding as she went.

"Did you hear what Mercedes said?" Taylor asked Prince Albert, who watched her attentively from his temporary holding stall. "If you let other people ride you, you'll get more to eat. And we all know how much you love to eat. I'll bring you some apples tomorrow; you, too, Pixie."

Taylor laid down fresh bedding, returned Prince Albert to his home, and then moved Pixie and worked on her stall. Taylor had just stopped to notice that a blister was forming between her thumb and forefinger when Mercedes returned, wearing her denim jacket. "Didn't you put work gloves on?" she questioned disapprovingly. She sighed and rolled her eyes when Taylor shook her head. "Next time bring work gloves. Who doesn't know that?"

"Me, I guess," Taylor admitted, feeling foolish.

"Come on. My mother's here. Like I said, she hates to wait."

Taylor quickly filled Pixie's and Prince Albert's feed buckets and then returned Pixie to her stall, shutting and locking the half door behind her. "Good night, you guys," she said as she dusted hay from her jeans and hair. "See you tomorrow. Be good."

As she passed the office where Mrs. LeFleur sat talking to someone on her cell phone, Taylor called good night and the ranch's owner beckoned her into the office. "I'm on the phone with a farrier," she told Taylor. "Pixie and Prince Albert need new shoes. I told him you'd be here next week on Wednesday when he comes. Is that all right?"

"Sure. I'm here that day."

"Excellent. Do you know any good vets? They're going to need checkups."

"No, but Daphne or Mercedes might, or I could ask Claire."

"You could ask Mercedes on the way home," Mrs. LeFleur suggested.

"Okay." A car horn sounded, prompting Taylor to get moving.

"See you tomorrow," Taylor said, leaving Mrs. LeFleur. At the wide front door, Taylor hesitated. What had she forgotten? There was nothing she could think of, but, still . . . the feeling nagged at her.

Chapter 10

"Come on!" Mercedes called. She stood beside a silver Acura with its motor running. Inside, a petite, stylish, dark-haired woman drummed perfectly manicured nails impatiently on the steering wheel.

Taylor ran toward the elegant car, suddenly feeling way too sweaty and messy to climb in. She was relieved to see that a blanket covered the backseat where she slid in beside Mercedes.

Mercedes introduced Taylor to her mother, who simply nodded and asked, "Where do you live?"

"Mrs. LeFleur asked if you know of a good horse vet," Taylor remembered to mention.

Mrs. Gonzalez snorted disdainfully as she pulled out onto Wildwood Lane. "Not around here."

"The only ones we know are back in Connecticut," Mercedes explained. "Daphne might know, though. Is something wrong with Prince Albert or Pixie?"

"No. She just wants them to be checked."

"Do you know anything about those animals?" Mrs. Gonzalez asked. "What's their lineage?"

Taylor held the ownership papers but that was all she knew. "I'm pretty sure Prince Albert is a quarter horse, and Pixie is a Shetland pony," she offered.

"Who's the sire?" Mrs. Gonzalez asked.

"His name is Prince Albert, not Sir Albert," Taylor answered.

Mercedes giggled and Taylor looked at her sharply, raising her eyebrows into a quizzical expression that asked what was so funny. "The sire is the father," Mercedes whispered. "Do you know the name of Prince Albert's father?"

"Oh," Taylor whispered back, feeling stupid. "No, I don't know his father," she said to Mrs. Gonzalez. "Or the mother."

"You'd better get them," said Mrs. Gonzalez. "You'll have a difficult time ever selling him or the pony without knowing their lineage."

Good, thought Taylor. *Then I'll never sell them.*

"We can get in touch with the state quarter horse association," Mercedes suggested. "If Prince Albert is pure quarter horse, he's probably registered. There's a half-blood association, too. If he's the product of two different purebred horses, he might be registered there."

Taylor didn't care if Prince Albert or Pixie were purebred or mixed with ten different breeds. What did it matter? They were both one of a kind to her.

The rest of the ride passed in near silence. The two tired girls listened to the radio and gazed out at the half-moon as the car glided up the steep and winding Quail Ridge Road.

All the way home, Taylor kept trying to remember what she had forgotten, but nothing came to her.

"I got your phone message saying you were going to the ranch, but I didn't expect you to be this late," Taylor's mother complained when she walked into the kitchen ten minutes later. "Your supper's cold, but I'll stick it into the microwave for you."

"Sorry," Taylor mumbled, though she really wasn't. She'd let her mother know where she was. What more did she expect?

Taylor sat down with her plate of warmed spaghetti and meatballs and told her mom all about Shafir and how Mrs. LeFleur was going to pass up a possibly great deal because she didn't want to deal with Mrs. Ross.

Jennifer clapped her hand to her forehead. "Oh! Don't remind me of Mrs. Ross. The luncheon is this Saturday afternoon, and I'm a wreck over it. Every time I think I've selected the perfect menu I begin to doubt myself. Maybe it's not good enough? What if her fancy friends expect caviar or foie gras or whatever those people eat?"

"I don't even know what that stuff is," Taylor remarked, wiping sauce from her mouth with the back of her hand.

Jennifer handed her a napkin. "Don't do that," she chided absently. "Caviar is fish eggs, and foie gras is goose liver."

"Ew, gross." Taylor wrinkled her nose.

"Oh, it doesn't matter what I serve, it's not going to be right."

"Why don't you check with Mrs. Ross?" Taylor suggested.

Jennifer considered this. "No," she decided. "I don't want her to know that it's Tuesday and I still don't have any idea what I'm serving. She just said, 'Surprise me and make it wonderful.' How should I know what she thinks is wonderful?"

Taylor got up and brought her empty plate to the sink. "Don't freak, Mom. Your food is great, and everyone will love it. They always do."

Jennifer looked at her and smiled. "Thanks, honey. Don't leave that dish in the sink. Put it in the dish-washer."

Taylor shifted her plate and silverware to the dish-washer. "Do you talk to Mrs. Ross much?" she asked as the seed of a new plan began to stir deep in the fertile soil of her mind.

"Occasionally," Jennifer said, beginning to page through one of the cookbooks piled on the table.

"What's she like?"

"Nice enough, I guess. Very businesslike. Scary."

"Scary?" Taylor questioned. "How is she scary?"

"I don't know," Jennifer said, her eyes still on the cookbook. "She doesn't smile much. And she's so rich and all. Rich people aren't like us."

"That's not true," Taylor protested. "They're only people. It's crazy to say they're not like us."

"I suppose so," Jennifer allowed with a shrug. "They seem different to me."

"Different isn't the same as scary," Taylor pressed.

Jennifer looked up from the cookbook. "I guess Mrs. Ross isn't really very friendly. All business, like I said."

"But she's not mean, right?"

"I don't know! She hasn't been mean to me — at least not yet."

"Why do you say not yet?" Taylor's voice had taken on a squeak of panic. Her plan would go so much more smoothly if Mrs. Ross wasn't mean.

"I'm just nervous about the luncheon. I'm afraid she'll be mad at me if it doesn't turn out well."

"Oh, I bet she'll be very nice about it — not that it will go badly, because it definitely won't. It'll be great, I'm sure."

"Why are you so interested in Mrs. Ross?" Jennifer asked, her brows knit in a perplexed expression.

"Just because I was over there today," Taylor replied. "I saw her riding."

"It's beautiful there, isn't it?"

Taylor nodded. "Could I help you on the day of the luncheon?" she volunteered.

"Taylor, we've been through this. You want to be paid, and I can't afford to pay you."

"No! I've changed my mind. I'll help you just to help you."

Jennifer squinted suspiciously at Taylor.

"Really! I liked it over there. I want to go back."

"You'll be working all day, not riding," Jennifer reminded her.

"I know. That's okay."

"All right, then."

Mrs. Ross would be at the luncheon. Maybe Taylor could slip away and speak to her about selling Shafir to Wildwood Stables.

Did she have the nerve to do it?

Taylor didn't know if she did.

But then Taylor never would have thought she'd be able to move a horse and pony through the woods to a home she'd found or convince Mrs. LeFleur to open Wildwood Stables. Doing these things had given her new confidence, greater than she had ever felt before. Maybe she was capable of more than she'd ever realized.

Perhaps she could speak to Mrs. Ross.

Still, the idea of it made her quake inside. Everyone regarded Mrs. Ross as such a powerful person.

"What are you thinking about?" Jennifer asked. "You suddenly look pale."

"Oh, nothing," Taylor told her. "I'd better go get that homework done."

In her bedroom, Taylor kicked off her shoes and flopped onto her mattress with her school backpack and did her homework. When she was done an hour later, she lay among her books, thinking about the day that had just passed. She recalled playing the game in the field with the horses. Maybe she could teach Prince Albert to play.

Taylor drifted off to sleep, still dressed. She awoke in the darkness. There was a blanket over her, and her books wcrc neatly stacked on her night table. The red LED light of her alarm clock showed 3:20 a.m.

Taylor suddenly sat up in bed. She remembered the thing she'd been trying to recall. She'd completely forgotten to go over to Travis's house.

Chapter 11

Why didn't you call me to find out why I wasn't there?" Taylor asked Travis the next day on the bus.

"Why should I?" Travis asked sulkily.

"I might have been thrown from a horse and sent to the hospital. You didn't know."

They were turning into PV Middle School too soon. Taylor didn't want the bus ride to end until Travis at least said that he understood and wasn't angry with her. He'd kept his head buried in his X-Men graphic novel since she'd sat down in the seat next to his. "Don't be mad," she coaxed. "I didn't know I'd meet Shafir, and I got so excited about the idea of her going to Wildwood Stables that I forgot about everything else."

"I'm not mad," Travis said, not looking at her.

"You're acting mad," Taylor pointed out.

"I'm not. George Santos came over. We did Wii Sports and he stayed for supper. I sort of forgot you were even coming over. That's why I never called."

"You forgot?" Taylor asked. A wave of relief swept over her. Her offense didn't seem as great if Travis had forgotten she was even supposed to come by. But that sense of being let off the hook was quickly overtaken by a different, unpleasant feeling.

"Did you have fun with George?" she asked cautiously.

"Yeah, it was great."

"Does he play Wii Bowling as well as I do?"

"Better. I can always beat you. I can't beat him."

"You can't always beat me."

"Can, too."

Travis turned the page of his graphic novel while Taylor sat scowling at him. "You are, too, mad," she insisted a few minutes later.

"I'm not mad. I forgot all about you."

A lump formed in Taylor's throat, but she used will-power to force it down. "I said I was sorry."

"Whatever," Travis said as the bus pulled in front of the school building. "It doesn't matter."

"Today is one of my afternoons to be at Wildwood Stables," Taylor said. "Why don't you bring your tools down? There's a stall door that needs to have its lock fixed."

Travis stood waiting for the departing students to leave and the aisle to clear. "George and I made plans to go to the skate park this afternoon," he said.

"But you're in charge of buildings and stuff at Wildwood," Taylor reminded him.

Travis just shrugged as he moved into the aisle.

"You're mad," Taylor said quietly with grim assurance, following Travis out of the bus.

Taylor came alongside Mr. Romano, her social studies teacher, as they were both about to enter her last period classroom that afternoon. "Hey, Taylor. How's my favorite place coming along?" he asked.

Taylor had told Mr. Romano how she needed to find

a home for Pixie and Prince Albert. He'd been the one who first mentioned the old Wildwood Stables to her. After her father also brought it up, Taylor had decided to go looking for it.

"Soon you'll be able to take your daughter there to ride," Taylor told Mr. Romano.

"She's only three."

"I'll take her for a pony ride on Pixie."

"That would be great. I can't wait to see the old place again," Mr. Romano said, smiling fondly. "Wildwood was such a big part of my childhood."

"Are you talking about Wildwood Stables?" asked Plum, coming alongside them.

"Yes, do you know it?" Mr. Romano answered Plum.

"I totally know it. I'm going to lease a horse that's there," Plum replied brightly. Turning to Taylor, she flashed a tight, nasty smile of victory and went quickly back to Mr. Romano. "He's a little difficult, but I know how to whip him into shape."

Taylor felt so enraged that her breath caught in her throat.

Mr. Romano caught sight of Taylor's wide-eyed fury.

"We'd better get into class," he said, guiding Plum in ahead of him so that he was between them.

"She's *not* getting him," Taylor hissed into Mr. Romano's back.

Taylor rode her bike to Wildwood Stables that afternoon. When she got there, she leaned it against the old maple with gnarled, aboveground roots that stood beside the first horse corral, and she watched as Daphne opened the back of a horse trailer. A man in jeans and a blue sweater who looked like he could be Daphne's father helped her set up a ramp at the back end.

In a few minutes, Daphne disappeared into the trailer and came out again leading Mandy, with the lunge line attached to Mandy's halter. The gray barb wore a yellow horse rug with red-and-green stripes. Her ankles were wrapped in blue horse boots, and the top of her tail, called the dock, was covered in a blue horse bandage. Taylor knew these things were just for protection while traveling.

When Mandy had stepped fully out of the trailer she hesitated on the ramp.

Mercedes came out of the main building and hurried over to the trailer. Taylor joined them, too. "Why is she stopping? Is she scared?" Taylor asked.

"I don't think she's really scared," Daphne replied. "She's just looking around, trying to figure out where she is."

"Give her a minute," Mercedes advised. "She'll come when she's ready."

Taylor nodded in agreement. Even bossy Mercedes was patient enough to let Mandy find her way in her own time. Taylor could just picture Plum dragging Mandy with the lead line or pulling on a chain shank.

Mandy lifted her head and sniffed the air. Her head turned toward Prince Albert and Pixie grazing in the field. The mare's ears swiveled toward them with keen interest. Daphne stroked Mandy's neck. "There are some friends for you," she said.

"I guess it's like being the new kid in a new school," Mercedes surmised. "Way scary! I should know."

Most of the kids in Pheasant Valley had been together since kindergarten. They'd known each other forever. They were even familiar with the students in the older and younger grades whom they didn't know as well. So, the fact that she was new in town made Mercedes an oddity. Taylor had asked her why her family had moved — she didn't think of it as an overly personal question — but Mercedes had never wanted to talk about it.

Mr. Chang looked at his watch. "I have to get this trailer back to the rental place and get to work," he remarked.

Taylor reached into her pocket for the cellophane bag of baby carrots she'd grabbed from the refrigerator on her way out. "I could lure her down with these," she suggested.

"That will do the trick. She loves them," Daphne said, "but be careful of your fingers. She loves them a little too much."

Taylor took out a carrot and approached the ramp. Staying at the bottom, she placed the orange morsel in her flattened palm and extended it to Mandy. The nervous mare caught the scent and stepped toward Taylor. "You know me," Taylor reminded her in a friendly tone. "We played in the field yesterday."

Mandy stepped down until she was close enough to snap up the small carrot with her tongue. Taylor stepped back, wiped her wet hand on her jeans, and then presented another carrot. This brought Mandy all the way off the ramp. "Good girl," she praised Mandy, petting her mane.

Mr. Chang hurriedly pulled the ramp away from the trailer and locked up. "See you tonight," he told Daphne, planting a kiss on her cheek. "I left your tack box inside."

"Okay. Thanks, Dad," Daphne said, waving as he drove the trailer away.

"She's a great-looking horse," Mercedes commented.

"Thanks," Daphne said. "I'm going to saddle her up and take her to the field to let her meet Pixie and Prince Albert."

Daphne led Mandy into the stable. "Want to walk up and meet them?" Taylor asked Mercedes.

"Okay." They headed toward the field behind a rect-angular paddock. The place seemed quiet today because no one was hammering or sawing. When Taylor men-tioned this, Mercedes sighed. "I don't think the workers are coming back. Mrs. L. is out of money."

"All her money?" Taylor questioned. If she had no money left, how would she pay for Shafir?

Mercedes shrugged. "I don't know. I just heard her arguing with the carpenter, who wanted to be paid today."

As soon as Mercedes and Taylor entered the field, Prince Albert and Pixie headed for them. "They smell those carrots," Mercedes said.

"From all the way over there?"

Mercedes nodded. "They have an unbelievable sense of smell."

"If there's food around, Prince Albert will find it," Taylor said with a laugh.

When Prince Albert and Pixie were near, Taylor took the carrots from her pocket and handed them to Mercedes. "Why don't you try feeding Prince Albert?" she suggested.

"Me?" Mercedes questioned. "He only likes you."

Taylor shifted from side to side. "Yeah, but he also loves to eat. He might not be able to resist if you offer him carrots. He likes them as much as he likes apples — which is a lot. If he takes food from you, maybe he'll let you ride him after a while."

"And you'd be okay with that?"

The question hit a sore point, but Taylor nodded. "He has to let other people ride him."

Prince Albert took the carrot from Mercedes without any hesitation. Taylor petted and praised him while Mercedes gave some of the carrots to Pixie.

"So far so good," Mercedes said, "but I wonder if he'd be as comfortable with me if you weren't here. I'm going to feed him some more while you back away."

With a nod of agreement, Taylor stopped stroking Prince Albert. When Mercedes offered him the carrot, he gobbled it eagerly. Taylor began to drift toward the back of the field. She had put about three yards between herself and Prince Albert when he noticed the space between them. With a longing glance at the carrot Mercedes offered, he turned away from it and walked to catch up with Taylor. As always, where Prince Albert went, Pixie followed.

"Now, that's love! He loves you more than food," Mercedes cried.

Taylor laughed, but a little sadly. She adored that Prince Albert was so devoted to her, but she hated to think what that love and devotion might cost him.

Chapter 12

$\mathcal{A}$t the end of the day on Thursday, Taylor was at her locker packing up when Plum and a group of her friends came down the hall. As always, Plum was at the center of her crowd like a queen bee, talking loud enough for all to hear. "Last night my mother spoke to the woman who owns the ranch. She told Mom that no one can ride that horse so he wouldn't be a good lease, but Mom assured her that I can get any horse to behave."

Taylor's words blurted forth before she could think about them. "I can ride him. He behaves just fine for me."

Plum turned slowly toward her. "Was I speaking to you?" she asked coldly. "No, I wasn't."

"What you were saying isn't true. I can ride him — but only me," Taylor insisted as Plum and her friends eyed her with disdain.

"Then the horse needs to be broken of that nasty habit," Plum said icily. With a nearly imperceptible nod, she ushered her crowd forward down the hall, leaving Taylor to fume in silent rage.

Taylor saw Travis coming toward her and was glad to see a friendly face. "You won't believe what just happened," she said when he was close enough to hear her.

"Plum again?" he asked.

"Who else?"

"I figured," he said. There was something in his tone that annoyed Taylor. It was as if he were bored with the subject.

"I'll tell you about it on the bus," she continued as she gathered the books she needed and shut her locker.

"I'm not taking the bus. George got me to join the computer club with him, and it meets this afternoon."

Taylor gazed at him with a blank expression as this new information sank in. Travis and she always sat together on the bus. Always! "You didn't tell me you were joining the computer club," was all she could think of to say. Travis usually told her everything.

He shrugged.

"How come you didn't ask if I wanted to join, too?" she pressed.

"I figured you're busy with the horse stuff."

"I asked you to do the horse stuff *with* me," Taylor reminded him, a slight, unwelcome shake of emotion coming into her voice.

"I know, but I'm not really about horses, ya know. And I don't think you love computers."

"I don't love them, but they're interesting and you could have asked."

"Then do you want to come?" he offered with a complete lack of enthusiasm.

"Not when you ask like that!"

Travis let out an exasperated sigh. "I have to go," he said. Glancing up the hall, Taylor saw George, a hefty, dark-haired boy, waiting for Travis.

"Whatever," Taylor said, dismissing the subject. "Are you coming to the ranch on Friday afternoon? We could really use your help."

"Maybe. I don't know."

"Come on. You said you would," Taylor insisted.

Travis began walking toward George. "I might come — if I remember."

When Taylor got home that afternoon, her mother was at the kitchen table. Sitting across from her was a petite woman with large brown eyes and chestnut hair cut to her chin, wearing jeans and a sweatshirt. Taylor wasn't surprised to see her because she'd spotted Claire Black's beat-up van parked in the driveway.

"Hey, ho, Taylor," Claire greeted her.

"How was school today?" her mother asked.

Taylor flattened her palm and twisted it from side to side. "Some good. Some bad. The usual."

Claire's brindle-coated pit bull, Bunny, came out from under the table to lick the back of Taylor's hand. Smiling, Taylor scratched her between the ears. "When you got Prince Albert's ownership papers from that woman, did she tell you anything about Prince Albert's or Pixie's background?" Taylor asked Claire.

"No," Claire replied. "I guess I should have asked. She told me Albert's all quarter horse and Pixie's a Shetland, but you'd already figured that out. Why do you want to know?"

"Mercedes's mother said we should know their lineage."

"It would tell us exactly how old they are, I suppose. When I get a minute, I'll call the sheriff and ask if he has an address for the old owner. Now I have a question for you," Claire said. "Is the ranch set up for lessons yet?"

"Yeah, Daphne brought her horse over just yesterday. She's going to use her for lessons."

"Not Prince Albert?"

Taylor explained the problem to Claire.

"You're probably the first person who's been kind to him in a long time," Claire said. "I can understand that he's having trouble trusting anyone else."

"We're trying to get him to allow other people to ride him so Mrs. LeFleur can use him as a school horse." She decided not to go into the additional problem of Plum, not wanting to even talk about it.

"Well, I was on a call about an opossum living in someone's basement today, and I started talking to the woman in the house while I set the Havahart trap," Claire explained. Taylor pictured the baited wire cages that

Claire always used to remove an animal without hurting it. "I told her about Wildwood, and she'd like to have her daughter start coming down," Claire continued. "She's been going online and talking to other parents of autistic children and she's been reading about horse therapy. She's located a therapist who will work with her."

"I have a cousin who has autism," her mom said. "You've never met him, Taylor. He's sort of in his own world, has trouble communicating. He doesn't follow directions well. His intelligence is actually pretty high, though."

"Are those, like, the kids who have aides with them in school?" Taylor asked.

"Sometimes," Claire confirmed. "Some autistic kids just need a little extra help to keep them on track, some need a lot of help. Anyway, this girl's therapist would like her to start doing some horse therapy, so I suggested Wildwood as a place where they might work. She's going to call Mrs. LeFleur."

"Cool," Taylor said. "Mrs. L. will be happy for the business. What's horse therapy?"

"Not sure," Claire admitted. "I guess you'll find out."

"Guess so," Taylor agreed. She decided that later she would text Daphne to give her the good news. This would be their first customer. Daphne had brought a few younger kids by, but they couldn't ride because Prince Albert wouldn't let them. Now that Daphne had brought Mandy over, maybe they would come back. With lots of luck, Wildwood Stables might really start to do business.

"Hey, I hear we're going to be working together Saturday," Claire said. "I'm helping your mom at the Ross River luncheon, and she says you are, too."

"Thank you both so much for volunteering to help," Jennifer said. "I really need a hand."

"Not a problem," Claire assured her.

Jennifer stood and opened the refrigerator. "I want you guys to try this onion dip I concocted. Tell me if it's any good." She set out a bowl of the dip and then returned to the refrigerator. "I'm serving the dip with a veggie platter," she explained as she rummaged through the packed fridge. "Now, where could those baby carrots be?"

"Oops," Taylor murmured.

Jennifer turned from the refrigerator to face her. "Oops, what?" she asked warily.

"I kind of fed them to the horses yesterday," Taylor squeaked.

"Taylor!" Jennifer scolded.

"Sorry," Taylor said, backing out of the kitchen. "Sorry!"

Chapter 13

On Friday, Taylor didn't press her hand brakes as she careened down the steep, winding hill leading to Wildwood Stables. Instead, she lifted from the seat and kept her speed up when she saw the street sign that read WILDWOOD LANE. She noticed that someone had pulled off all the vines that had once obscured the sign from view. Taylor had mixed feelings about that. She wanted to keep her special, magical place all to herself, but she knew it had to open to the public in order for it to survive — which meant people had to be able to find it.

Taylor turned a sharp left at the sign and then careered past the overgrown forsythia bushes into the dirt road. The ruts and bumps caused her teeth to clack together as they slowed her down. The first thing she noticed as she rode into the ranch was that the chipped, faded sign that had once stood there — that was too weathered to even read — had been removed. She wondered if Mrs. LeFleur was planning to replace it.

Daphne and Mrs. LeFleur stood in the center of the nearest corral. Mandy was there, though she was not tacked up for riding. With them were two women Taylor didn't recognize. One was a heavyset blonde and the other was strong looking and wiry, with dark curly hair and dark skin.

Curious to know what was happening, Taylor settled her bike against the tree and hopped over the corral fence. "Here's our Taylor," Mrs. LeFleur said warmly. She introduced Taylor and then explained that the blonde woman was Alice, the person with the autistic daughter whom Claire had told Taylor about. The other woman was Lois, the therapist.

"I have a degree in psychology, but I'm still in the process of getting my certification in horse therapy at the state university," Lois explained. "Alice is allowing me to use her daughter for my final certification presentation."

She held up a small video camera. "Would one of you be able to film my work with Dana?"

"Dana is my seven-year-old," Alice explained.

"I was hoping you would do it, Taylor," said Mrs. LeFleur.

"Sure," Taylor agreed, taking the camera from Lois. "Where's Dana?"

"She went into the stable to look at the other two horses," Alice said. "I'll go get her."

While Alice was gone, Lois explained to them that she wouldn't try to get Dana up on Mandy right away. "I'm going to start with having her get used to the horse, then lead her and take her through the most basic commands. We find that children who have trouble focusing and staying on task are often so engaged by the beauty and size of a horse that they tend to stay interested longer than usual. Also, having mastery over such a large animal gives them tremendous self-esteem and confidence."

Mercedes came out of the main building holding a long stick with a loop at its end. "This is what you're looking for, isn't it?" she asked Lois, handing it to her.

"Yes. This is called a wand, right?"

"It is," Daphne confirmed.

Alice emerged from the main building with Dana, a pale, fragile-looking blonde. She reminded Taylor of a little yellow canary, delicate and ready to fly away at the first fright. Alice guided Dana into the corral and brought her to Mandy. "This is the horse you're going to be working with, honey," Alice said to her daughter.

Dana's eyes went wide and she scowled. The girl folded her arms and shook her head forcefully back and forth.

"But she's a nice horse, sweetie," Alice pressed.

"She's very gentle," Daphne put in.

"Nooo!" Dana shouted, and then raced back to the main building, disappearing inside.

"What should I do?" Alice asked, looking to Lois.

Lois began walking toward the main building, after Dana. "Let me go try to see what the matter is. Give me about ten minutes and then come in."

"Is it ten minutes yet?" Alice asked the group as they waited in the corral. Mrs. LeFleur checked her watch and nodded. But before Alice had a chance to move, Lois emerged from the main building and rejoined them.

"Dana wants a different horse," Lois said. "That black horse in the stable."

"That's Prince Albert," Taylor told Lois.

"Well, for some reason, that's the one she wants. Could we work with Prince Albert?"

"Prince Albert is a one-gal horse," Mrs. LeFleur explained. "Taylor is the only one he'll let ride him."

"But you said Dana wasn't going to ride today, right?" Taylor pointed out.

"Yes, but eventually she will," Lois said.

"We're working with him. Maybe by the time Dana is ready Prince Albert will be ready, too." Taylor didn't want this chance to show Mrs. LeFleur how useful Albert could be to slip away.

Taylor cut her eyes to Daphne, looking for support, and Daphne got her message. "And Taylor is here, which should make Prince Albert comfortable. He's really a very gentle horse," she said.

"Very gentle," Taylor echoed.

Without further discussion, they all moved toward the main building, which housed Prince Albert's stable. They entered and walked down the shadowy central aisle — past the office, the tack room, and empty box stalls — to the back two stalls. "Look at that," Mercedes murmured. "How sweet."

Dana was standing in front of Prince Albert's stall. She rested her forehead on Prince Albert's muzzle and stroked it gently while Pixie looked on from her stall.

"Is he always so patient with children?" Lois asked.

Taylor was tempted to say that he was amazing with kids, but she decided to stick with the truth. "We've never seen him interact with kids," she admitted.

"I wonder why she likes him better than Mandy," Mercedes said. "Mandy is a good, steady horse, too."

"Maybe she sees something in his eyes," Taylor suggested, speaking on impulse. The moment the words were out of her mouth, she knew she was right. There was something in the horse's eyes that she also sensed. It was hard to describe. What was it? He'd known suffering. Was it sadness? No. That wasn't really what Taylor sensed; at least it wasn't only sadness. It was more than that. Perhaps it was sadness combined with a quiet strength and a strong spirit. And she saw kindness there in Prince Albert's dark, soulful eyes, too. Taylor felt certain that these were the qualities that Dana was responding to.

When they were close to Dana, the little girl turned

her head toward them, resting her ear on Prince Albert's muzzle. Taylor noticed that she didn't look at any of them directly and remembered her mother saying that people with autism had difficulty with communicating. "This is a good horse," Dana said. "He likes me."

"I'll get a halter and lead line," Taylor volunteered. She sprinted to the tack room, found what she needed, and quickly returned. Once the halter was on, she led Prince Albert out of his stall. "Would you like to get to know him better outside?" Taylor asked Dana.

The little girl's face became radiant with happy excitement. She nodded vigorously.

"Can I give her the lead line?" Taylor checked with Lois.

"Would you like to lead him out?" Lois asked Dana.

Dana's eyes grew large. "I could do that?"

"Sure," Taylor said. "I'll walk beside you." She handed the line to Dana and then clicked softly, signaling Prince Albert to move forward. "Walk on, Prince Albert," Taylor commanded calmly. "We're going outside."

From her stall, Pixie whinnied. "She doesn't like Prince Albert to leave her behind," Taylor explained to the group. "It makes her very nervous."

"She's going to have to get over that," Mercedes commented.

"Let's bring her along for now," Mrs. LeFleur suggested. "Mercedes, would you attend to that, please? Join us in the corral once she's haltered."

"Okay," Mercedes agreed, heading for the tack room.

Outside, Mrs. LeFleur held the corral gate open for Taylor and Dana to lead Prince Albert in. The rest of the group followed. "Let Dana lead Prince Albert around the ring by herself now," Lois instructed. "And, if you don't mind, get the video recorder and film her doing it."

Taylor hesitated. If Prince Albert sidestepped or balked, she wanted to be right there to get him back on track. As if sensing her reluctance, Daphne moved in closer to take Taylor's place near Prince Albert.

"Dana will be fine," Lois assured them with a smile. "You're okay, aren't you, Dana?"

Dana's rapturous smile was still firmly on her face as she nodded a definite yes.

"Good," said Lois. "When you've taken him a full circle around, bring him back to me."

Taylor had set the video camera down on the picnic bench outside the corral and she scrambled over the fence

108

to get it. She was soon back and trailing Dana, filming her every move.

As they went, Dana kept her head down and wouldn't look at Taylor, even though Taylor kept giving her words of encouragement. When they had made it all the way around, Dana led Prince Albert to Lois.

Lois showed Dana the wand Mercedes had brought out for her. "You're going to use this to make the horse turn," Lois told the girl. "It's not to scare or hit Prince Albert; it's only to guide him. All right?"

"It sort of makes your arm longer," Taylor explained.

Dana still didn't look at anyone, but Taylor noticed that the girl was gazing up at Prince Albert. It seemed to Taylor as though Dana was most comfortable in her own private world, yet for some reason, she had decided to allow this gentle, large black quarter horse into that world.

In the next hour, Lois had Dana move Prince Albert in a circle holding the wand at his hindquarters as a guide. Mercedes and Daphne set up a simple obstacle course using items they found in the tack room and the storage shed behind the washhouse. With Prince Albert still on a lead line, Dana walked him through the course. All the while, Taylor filmed Dana and Prince Albert, and the rest watched the little girl and horse as they offered encouragement and praise.

Taylor was so proud of her horse and happy to be filming him at his best. In the sunlight, framed by the camera, she was aware of how his ribs jutted out from his hungry days of abandonment and his coat still had no shine, probably because he was still recovering from malnourishment. Pixie had these problems, too.

But Taylor had found them a good home where they were being properly fed and exercised. She vowed anew to make sure nothing interfered with this wonderful new life they now had. Nothing.

Chapter 14

"Are the fruit cups out on the buffet?" Jennifer asked Taylor on Saturday morning. They were in the large, gleaming stainless-steel kitchen of Mrs. Ross's mansion. Her sprawling home was tucked into a wooded glade at the back of Ross River Ranch.

"I just put them out," said Claire, coming into the room with an empty tray.

"Don't just stand there, Taylor," Jennifer scolded mildly. "Put that silverware in the baskets and get them out there on the table."

"Okay," Taylor murmured. She knew she was not being as helpful as she should be. But Taylor had never seen a place like this, and she felt awed by its grandeur —

crystal chandeliers, golden fixtures, sky-high ceilings, glistening many-paned windows that rose three stories in places! It was more like a palace than a home.

"Right now, Taylor," Jennifer prompted. "Please stop daydreaming and snap to it."

"Sorry. Okay." Taylor began unloading the utensils Jennifer had rented into three woven baskets, sorting the knives, forks, and spoons into their own baskets. When she was done, she carried them out the kitchen door and into a big, sunny room that had been set up with four large round tables. Taylor put the baskets down near the stack of white luncheon plates at the end of a long, rectangular table.

Taylor stood there drinking in the grandness of the room. Unable to resist, she moved into its middle to experience the sensation of having so much space around her. She imagined how it must feel to be Devon Ross, the queen of all this, and a feeling of power suffused her. It was a little frightening but exciting, too.

"Weren't you riding Cody the other day?"

Taylor swung around to face the tall, lean, dark-haired woman who had spoken to her. Devon Ross's delicate, fine-boned face was neutral, neither welcoming nor angry.

She was dressed in a brown pantsuit with an emerald green satin blouse. Her straight hair was pulled back severely into a twisted bun.

Taylor opened her mouth to reply, but no sound came out. Her mind was still too busy dealing with the unlikely fact that she was actually standing face-to-face with Devon Ross.

"That was you I saw on Cody, was it not?" Mrs. Ross queried once more.

Taylor nodded. "Yes, that was me. I hope it was all right. My friend told me he needed to be ridden, for the exercise."

"Do you board here?" Mrs. Ross asked.

"No, I was with my friend Daphne Chang. She boards here; well, she did until this month, anyway."

"Oh, yes, I heard something about that. She took Mandy over to the new horse ranch, the one that was closed for so many years."

"Wildwood Stables," Taylor supplied.

"Yes, that's what it used to be called. I had my people bid on it to use as extra room, but something went wrong with the deal. I forget what." She studied Taylor, looking her up and down. "What brings you here?"

"I'm helping my mother. She's in the kitchen."

"I see. How did you like Cody?"

"He's wonderful! I liked him a lot."

"You rode him well. Watching you out in the field reminded me of my daughter, Leslie. I originally bought Cody for her, but she's a grown woman now and doesn't get back to ride him very often."

"That's too bad," Taylor said.

Mrs. Ross became thoughtful. "Yes, well, that's what happens to little girls and boys; they grow up and develop their own ideas about things. It's annoying, really."

Taylor had no idea how to respond, and she was relieved that her mother chose that very moment to come hurrying out of the kitchen door, searching the room.

"Taylor, what in the world is taking —" Jennifer cut herself short when she saw Mrs. Ross.

Mrs. Ross walked toward Jennifer. "It's entirely my fault. I was engaging her in conversation." Mrs. Ross and Jennifer returned to the kitchen together, going inside just as Claire was coming out with a tall coffee urn in her arms. "Taylor, help me figure out how to set this thing up," she said. "I have no idea how to use it."

Taylor joined her at the table. "Neither do I," she admitted.

"Was that who I think it was?" Claire asked as she pulled the top off the urn and stared into it.

Taylor nodded. "Uh-huh."

"What did her majesty have to say?" Claire asked. She glanced up at Taylor and smiled.

"She's not happy that her daughter grew up and moved away. She's annoyed that she has ideas of her own."

"Oh, poor thing," Claire joked, smiling wryly. "I guess all the money in the world can't stop that from happening."

"Is this where the equestrian society luncheon is being held?" asked a petite blonde woman coming into the room.

"It sure is. You're the first guest to arrive, so welcome, and please have a seat," Claire told her. From that moment on, Taylor was in a blur of activity — bringing out food, refilling dishes, pouring drinks, getting ice, collecting dirty dishes.

As she went back and forth, Taylor listened to the guest speaker. She was the same petite blonde who had first come in, and she was from the American Horse

Council. "When people encounter economic difficulties," she said, "they sell their boats, their vacation homes, and get rid of their horses — only a boat doesn't have feelings, and a horse does."

Taylor pictured Prince Albert's liquid brown eyes, so full of emotion.

"A tough economy requires horse owners to get smarter about how they spend. They have to cut back on shows, lessons, trailering, and other equipment," the speaker said.

Taylor made a mental note to tell Mrs. LeFleur what she was hearing. It seemed like it could be helpful.

"More than ever before," the speaker continued, "horses are being offered for adoption or dumped at auction. Many are being offered free lease by owners who cannot afford the upkeep, which in our state can range from three hundred fifty dollars a month for rough board to two thousand a month. The cost of an adequate supply of hay and grain to feed a thousand-pound horse is four hundred dollars a month."

Taylor set the plates she was holding down on a table and listened, mouth agape. She'd had no idea it was so expensive. Suddenly, she understood why her parents had been so against her keeping Prince Albert and Pixie. She also now realized why Mrs. LeFleur was so in favor of leasing Prince Albert.

Claire came up next to Taylor. "Don't let your mother see you standing there like that," she cautioned. "We have to start bringing out desserts."

By three o'clock Mrs. Ross was saying good-bye to her guests, and Taylor remembered what she'd come hoping to speak to her about: Shafir.

Did she have the nerve?

Taylor waited for a moment when Mrs. Ross was alone and then, wiping her greasy hands on her black pants, she approached. "Everything went so well," Mrs. Ross said when she noticed Taylor.

"Thanks. My mom will be really happy you feel that way," Taylor replied. "Mrs. Ross, there's an Arabian here that Daphne told me you were thinking of selling."

"Shafir?"

"Yes! That's her. How much do you want for her?"

"She's not trained."

"I could help Daphne train her."

Mrs. Ross stared at her quizzically. "Is it you or Daphne who wants her?"

"Both. Well, neither. Wildwood Stables is just starting up and needs horses. I was thinking maybe if Mrs. LeFleur who owns the place could —"

"Mrs. LeFleur inherited the place, am I correct?"

"Yes. If she could call you and —"

"I could get twenty thousand dollars for that horse if she were trained," Mrs. Ross said. "Untrained, she's still worth ten thousand, maybe fifteen."

These numbers staggered Taylor's mind. Fifteen thousand dollars for a horse!

"Do you know her lineage?" Taylor asked, remembering that Mercedes's mother had said a horse would be hard to sell without that. Her boldness shocked her. Had she actually found the nerve to say that? Taylor hoped she wasn't reddening with embarrassment and fought a strong urge to run away.

Mrs. Ross studied Taylor with an expression that fell somewhere between disbelief and amusement. "You're quite the horse trader, aren't you, young lady?"

"I'm just asking," Taylor replied with a sheepish grin.

"In fact, I had Shafir checked, and she's a papered purebred Arabian. I can provide the documentation."

"I don't think Mrs. LeFleur would care about the papers. She just wants a horse for lessons and trail rides."

"I caused Mrs. LeFleur a lot of trouble, though I didn't mean to. And Shafir is growing wilder by the day. Tell her the horse is hers."

"She might have to pay you a little at a time," Taylor suggested. Again she was aghast at how forward she was being. But, she was discovering, it thrilled her, too — made her feel capable and grown-up.

"No, I meant she can have the horse. I'd rather have someone training that gorgeous creature than have her ignored. I didn't pay anything for her, and she's costing me money. I'll have Bob Haynes trailer her over tomorrow in the morning."

"Really?" Taylor asked, hardly able to believe her luck.

Mrs. Ross smiled, but just a little. "I'm glad someone can use her."

Chapter 15

*E*arly Sunday morning, Taylor shivered a little in her fleece jacket as she rode her bike into Wildwood Stables. On Saturday she'd called Mrs. LeFleur, Daphne, and Mercedes and left messages about Shafir on all their phones. So far, no one had gotten back to her.

Mrs. Ross had only said that Shafir would arrive in the morning, but not exactly when. So Taylor had set her alarm for six a.m. so she could be at Wildwood by six-thirty.

Taylor went directly to the feed shed behind the main stable. She filled two buckets with oats and then went around the back to the old pump for some water. Setting a bucket under the spigot, she began priming the pump by cranking the handle up and down vigorously to get the water flowing.

Morning mist still blanketed the ground and rose from the forest just beyond, giving the ranch a soft glow. *This really is the best place in the world*, she thought as water began to pour, crystal clear and ice-cold, from the spout. Even the water was better than anywhere else.

Mrs. LeFleur was going to be so thrilled that Taylor had gotten a new horse for Wildwood Stables — and for free! Daphne and Mercedes might know more about horses, but she was the one who had gotten this much-needed addition to the stables.

Taylor carried the water into the stable and set it down. She wanted to let the icy water warm up a little so it wouldn't upset Prince Albert's and Pixie's stomachs. "Good morning," she greeted the horse and pony brightly. "You're going to have some new company today."

Prince Albert sputtered.

Taylor knew he wasn't really responding to her remark, but she pretended he had. "Well, she's a little wild, but I'm sure she'll settle down once Daphne works with her a bit. She likes to play and she's very friendly."

She had gone to get the oats when she heard the

engine of a trailer gliding to a stop in front of the main building. Walking around the corner of the building to the front, she saw a sleek silver trailer. A man with graying hair and a bit of a belly got out, looking around.

"Hi, I guess you're Bob Haynes," Taylor said as she approached. "I'm Taylor Henry."

"Hey, there. I was told to ask for Mrs. Flowers."

"LeFleur," Taylor corrected him. "She's not here, but I can take Shafir and put her in a stable."

"Do you work here?"

"Yes."

"I'd better wait for the owner."

At that moment, the sound of kicking and angry neighing came from the trailer.

"I had a heck of a time catching her this morning, and apparently she doesn't like to travel, either," Bob explained.

A dark green Volvo station wagon turned from Wildwood Lane into the ranch. Mrs. LeFleur parked off to the side and practically flew out of the car.

"Is the horse here already? Oh, dear, it is!" Mrs. LeFleur turned to Bob. "I'm sorry. You have to take this horse back. I can't possibly have it here."

"But, Mrs. LeFleur, this is a great gift," Taylor protested.

"She's right," Bob agreed. "A horse like Shafir would sell for upward of fifteen thou."

"Then why doesn't Devon Ross just sell her?" Mrs. LeFleur asked.

"I have no idea," Bob admitted.

Taylor turned toward Bob. "Could you wait just a few minutes while Mrs. LeFleur and I talk?" she requested.

"I can spare a few minutes, but then I've got to get going," he agreed.

As Taylor followed Mrs. LeFleur into the office, she hoped Daphne would show up soon. Convincing the ranch's owner that they could train Shafir would sound more believable if Daphne were the one saying it.

When they were inside the office, Mrs. LeFleur faced Taylor. "I know you meant well. Just the same, I cannot have another horse that I must feed and board but that I can't use for lessons."

"Wait until you see her, though. She's gorgeous."

"That she may be. Nonetheless —"

Mercedes practically flew, breathlessly, into the office. "Is she really an Arabian? I picked up your message late last night, and I came over as soon as I could. Why isn't she unloaded yet?"

"Mrs. LeFleur doesn't think we can use her," Taylor explained.

"She's an untrained horse," Mrs. LeFleur clarified.

"But a horse like that is worth a fortune!" Mercedes cried. "You can't turn her down. It's like throwing away a winning lottery ticket!"

"I can't use her, and yet I'll have to feed her, house her, pay for her farrier and veterinarian costs. An untrained horse is just a drain on my finances no matter how valuable she may be," Mrs. LeFleur insisted stubbornly.

"I can start her," Mercedes said confidently. "On our ranch back in Weston I started a Morgan gelding who was only four and super spirited."

"You had a Morgan?" Taylor asked.

"We had a bunch of horses."

Taylor was dying to know more about Mercedes's background, but she never seemed to want to talk about it too much. Her move to Pheasant Valley had obviously been a move down, in terms of wealth, and Mercedes clearly missed the stable of horses that her family no longer owned.

"Daphne is sure she can train Shafir, too," Taylor told Mrs. LeFleur, "and I'll work with both of them."

"While you're all also working with Prince Albert," Mrs. LeFleur reminded Taylor. "He still needs to tolerate a rider other than you."

"Yes, but you saw how great he was with Dana. Lois and Dana and her mother will be back to work with him again. That's like a riding lesson," Taylor said.

"What happens when they want to have Dana ride?" Mrs. LeFleur questioned.

"By then he'll know Dana and he'll let her on," Taylor proposed optimistically.

"You can't be sure of that," Mrs. LeFleur countered.

"By then we'll have Shafir ready to go," Mercedes put in. "Or we can use Mandy."

"But that little girl only wants Prince Albert," Mrs. LeFleur reminded them. "Besides, I don't trust that Mrs. Ross."

"She told me she was sorry if she caused you trouble over the ranch," Taylor said. "That was one of the reasons she wants you to have Shafir, to make up for it."

Taylor was unprepared for the redness that came to Mrs. LeFleur's face. "That woman thinks she can buy whatever she wants. Well, money will not buy my forgiveness."

Taylor and Mercedes looked at each other, taken aback by Mrs. LeFleur's passionate anger. Could such deep feeling be about a court case?

"Do you know Mrs. Ross personally?" Taylor dared to ask.

"Our paths have crossed before," Mrs. LeFleur revealed.

"What happened?" Taylor asked softly.

"I'd rather not discuss it," Mrs. LeFleur replied.

For a minute or more, no one spoke. The red fury left Mrs. LeFleur, though she still seemed shaken. Taylor waited until the woman appeared to be completely herself again before speaking. "It's not Shafir's fault that she keeps getting dumped on someone else. She needs a home."

Bob Haynes appeared at the door before Mrs. LeFleur could respond to Taylor. "What would you like me to do, Mrs. LeFleur?"

Chapter 16

By the time Daphne's father dropped her off at Wildwood, Prince Albert, Pixie, and Shafir were all in the corral along with Mercedes and Taylor.

"Oh, she's here! I can't believe you did it, Taylor!" Daphne said, swinging her legs over the corral fence. "Where's Mrs. L.?"

"She's gone to the office," Taylor replied. "I think she's in shock, but she agreed to keep Shafir."

"All right!" Daphne cheered.

"Do you know if she'll take a saddle and halter?" Mercedes asked Daphne.

"I don't think so. I've never seen her in one," Daphne

replied. "How is she dealing with Pixie and Prince Albert?"

"She's prancing around them, but they're kind of ignoring her," Taylor reported.

"At least they're not nipping her or being aggressive in any way," Mercedes pointed out.

"That's true. I think they'll be friends eventually, but for now, they need to get to know one another," Daphne said. "I'll bring Mandy out, too. They can all spend some time together. In another hour or so, we should see if we can get a rope halter on Shafir."

"Why not a regular halter?" Mercedes questioned.

"I just think they're lighter than a regular halter, which is good for a horse that isn't used to any kind of tack," Daphne explained. "There's a nylon rope halter in the tack room. If we can get Shafir to accept it, then we can start her training by just walking her around on a lead line at first."

"I'll do that," Mercedes volunteered.

"We should take turns," Daphne suggested. "That way she'll get used to all of us."

Mercedes appeared disappointed by Daphne's response, though she nodded in agreement. Taylor suspected that she missed having a horse of her own and was hoping to become Shafir's unofficial guardian — or at least the one Shafir knew and liked best. After all, Taylor had her bond with Prince Albert and even Pixie. Daphne had Mandy. But Mercedes didn't have a horse to call her own.

While Prince Albert, Pixie, and Shafir got to know one another in the corral, the girls used the time to get their chores done. Daphne got Mandy groomed and ready to go out. Taylor went to work on Pixie and Prince Albert's stalls. She gave them a thorough cleaning, removing all the straw bedding after picking out the droppings with a rake. She then hosed down each stall. While she was doing that she noticed a rough, splintery surface on the top of the half door to Prince Albert's stall.

Mercedes was down the center aisle sweeping. "Mercedes, would you take a look at this?" Taylor asked. When Mercedes joined her, she pointed to the rough patch.

"That wasn't there on Friday," Taylor said.

"Uh-oh," Mercedes said. "He might just be wood biting, but he could be cribbing."

"What's that?" Taylor asked.

"He made those marks with his teeth," Mercedes

explained. "Wood biting is chewing the wood and it's a bad habit, but cribbing is worse. Cribbing is when a horse holds on to a piece of wood with his front teeth and throws his head back to suck in air."

"Why would a horse do that?" asked Taylor.

"The rush of inhaled air feels good to a horse, and horses usually do it when they're stressed. Or just out of boredom."

"He's stressed?" Taylor questioned. "Why would he be stressed? Or bored? Everything is so much better for him now." Taylor felt deeply unsettled by the idea that Prince Albert might not be completely happy when it was her goal to give him a perfect life.

"He's probably bored. We have to stop him from cribbing right away," Mercedes said. "Once that behavior sets in, it's almost impossible to break the habit. Pixie might even start doing it."

"Is it dangerous?" Taylor asked.

"Yeah. It can make him real sick."

"What can we do about it?"

"We could get him a cribbing collar."

"Is that like those big cones dogs wear after they've had a surgery at the vet's?"

132

"Sort of," Mercedes confirmed.

"Prince Albert wouldn't like that. What else is there?"

"There's stuff we could put on his stall that tastes bad. We could cover the top of his stall door with metal, but he might just find something else to chomp on. You might try getting him a salt lick or maybe a horse toy so he won't be so bored."

Taylor went to the tack room and took out a bridle with a flexible D-ring snaffle bit. She was pulling down the ranch's new synthetic all-purpose saddle when Daphne came in and scooped a rope halter from its hook. "What happened? You look upset."

Taylor told Daphne about the marks on Albert's stall door and her conversation with Mercedes. "So, I don't really know what to do," she concluded. "I'm just going to take Prince Albert out for a ride now and think about it. What would you do?"

Daphne sighed thoughtfully, tapping the rope harness against her side. "Maybe Prince Albert needs to spend less time in his stall and more time turned out in the field. I can do that on the days you're not here. And — I don't know — maybe you could get here on a weekend day to ride him and make sure you give him a ride every time you are here."

"And do you think that would work?" Taylor asked.

"Try it, and then if it doesn't, we can think of something else," Daphne replied. "She's right that we should get him to stop cribbing. It's not good for him."

"Okay, thanks." Talking to Daphne had improved Taylor's mood. She felt less panicked, less guilty.

"Don't worry," Daphne said as she left the tack room. "We'll figure it out."

Taylor loaded all the tack she needed plus a helmet into a wheelbarrow and pushed it toward the corral, staggering a little under the weight of the saddle, pad, stirrups, and bridle. Letting herself into the corral, she clicked, and Prince Albert headed toward her, followed by Pixie. Once the horse was completely tacked, she swung into the saddle.

On the other side of the corral, Mercedes was trying to slip the rope halter over Shafir's head, but the spirited Arabian mare kept ducking away from her.

Daphne was approaching, leading Mandy.

"Could you open the gate for me?" Taylor requested.

Daphne pulled the corral gate open. "I'm going to teach you to do this yourself," Daphne said as Taylor and Prince Albert passed through at a walk, followed by Pixie.

"Okay," Taylor agreed. "That would be good." There were so many things about horses she wanted to learn; the list seemed endless, but she was eager to improve.

At the gate to the field, Taylor had to hop off, open the gate, lead Pixie and Prince Albert through, and then mount once again. Knowing how to open the gate from atop a horse really would be helpful, she decided.

With a light squeeze, all the command Prince Albert required, Taylor moved him into a lively trot, what she thought of as a jog. Behind them, Pixie automatically picked up her pace.

The field was a rounded, gently sloping mound. The sun was now well into the sky. Taylor reined Prince Albert back a moment so she could open her fleece jacket.

Prince Albert slowed at a sunny patch of yellow dandelions that had not yet turned into puffballs. He stretched his head down to munch on the vegetation, but Taylor gently pulled him back up. "No eating with your bridle still on!" she said, dismounting. "We don't need any more bad habits." Slipping off the bridle, she landed softly in the thick grass, trusting Prince Albert not to run off. She wasn't too worried since he was occupied with his favorite pastime — eating.

Taylor dismounted and sat cross-legged in the field. That put her just above eye level with the grazing Pixie and Prince Albert. "Why are you stressed, Albert?" Taylor asked, not really expecting an answer, but hoping that somehow he could sense her question. "I'm sorry if I haven't been paying attention to you this week. I've been really busy. You know, one minute I had all this time, and the next minute Claire asks me to go pick up an abandoned horse and pony with her, and just like that, my life is turned upside down! Suddenly, I work at a ranch and have all these responsibilities."

Lying back flat in the grass, Taylor gazed up at the vivid blue sky. Shutting her eyes, she let the red and orange swirls caused by the sun play across her eyelids.

Taylor wondered if Prince Albert had sensed any of what she had said to him. But how could she expect a horse to understand what she was dealing with when her own best friend didn't even seem to understand?

Had she done the same thing to Travis that she had unintentionally done to Prince Albert — made him feel unimportant and unappreciated?

Prince Albert whinnied anxiously. When Taylor opened her eyes, he was standing over her. Prince Albert stuck his nose out toward her and breathed softly onto her face, like Daphne had done to him before. Taylor smiled up into his soft, round eyes, knowing that it was his way of communicating with her.

Sitting forward, she stroked his muzzle. "I'm all right, boy. Sorry if I scared you." Taylor was so touched by Prince Albert's affection that emotional tears sprang to her eyes. Clasping his muzzle in both hands, she kissed its velvet surface.

As though not wanting to be left out, Pixie moved in close to them. Taylor laughed to see the sunny round weeds all jutting this way and that as Pixie held them in her mouth. In the next second, Pixie munched them down.

Getting to her feet, Taylor yanked up fistfuls of dandelion flowers. One by one, she snapped the stems short. Coming alongside Pixie, Taylor began tucking the dandelion flowers into Pixie's frizzy mane. "You haven't been getting much attention, either, have you?" she said gently as she decorated the coarse, wiry blonde hair. "But you never seem to mind."

Taylor thought about her father. Now that he'd moved out, she hardly ever saw him. He'd told her he was coming by this week, but here it was Sunday and he still hadn't shown. Did she feel hurt? Sure she did. It helped that she hadn't really believed he would come by — because he never did — but somewhere in the back of her mind she'd held out a small flicker of hope.

Was it the same for Prince Albert? Did he sit in his stall every day and hope Taylor would come? Were three out of seven days a week enough? Maybe in his mind it was not. She hated to think of him biting on his stall door anxiously, not knowing if she would arrive.

She would come to the barn more often, she decided.

But that would give her even less time to spend with Travis.

Chapter 17

Taylor got into the saddle and headed back toward the main building. As she got close, she could see that Mandy was grazing at a grassy corner inside the corral. Daphne was standing in the middle of the corral holding a long lead line that was looped around Shafir's neck, and she had the young mare walking in a circle. In Daphne's other hand, she held the wand that Dana had used the other day.

Pausing Prince Albert and Pixie just outside the corral, Taylor stopped to watch.

Daphne looked over at them and smiled. "Nice hairdo," she remarked with a nod at Pixie's flower-strewn mane.

"Thanks. Shafir wouldn't take the halter?"

"No," Daphne answered. "It was probably too soon for that, anyway. I'm just trying to get her to obey my voice commands right now. So far she only goes if I tap her with the wand as I click. She'll stop if I say 'whoa,' but only if I hold the wand in front of her."

"It sounds like a good way to start her on voice commands," Taylor commented.

"It's not bad for the first day," Daphne agreed.

"Where's Mercedes?" Taylor asked.

"Shafir turned abruptly and knocked her down."

"Is Mercedes okay?" Taylor asked.

"I don't think anything is broken, but she slid in the dirt and got some scrapes and bruises. She just threw the halter down and stomped off, so I guess she isn't in the best mood."

"Oh, dear," Taylor murmured. She was about to dismount when a black SUV drove into the ranch, going too fast before stopping abruptly. Beverly Mason got out at the same time Plum stepped from the passenger side. "That's him, Mom," Plum said, pointing to Prince Albert. "See, he can be ridden. She's riding him right now. Look!"

Taylor froze in the saddle for a moment, unprepared for Plum's sudden appearance. But she realized that she should have expected them. Mrs. LeFleur had told them to come back in a week, and the week was up. Was this it? Was Plum about to get her lease on Prince Albert?

Don't just sit there, say something! Taylor urged herself. "He's very difficult," she blurted after a moment. "I'm the only one who can handle him."

"I can handle him," Plum said, waving her off. "If he won't let me ride him at first, I'll get him to change his mind."

"Is Mrs. LeFleur here?" Beverly asked.

"No!" Taylor lied impulsively.

Plum and her mother looked at Taylor skeptically. "Whose car is that, then?" Plum asked, pointing at Mrs. LeFleur's green Volvo.

"Not sure," Taylor kept up the pretense. "I think one of the workers left it there."

Sensing the tension in Taylor's body, Prince Albert's ears flattened. His tail swished, a sure sign of aggressive behavior.

"See how he is?" Taylor said, desperately searching for anything that would put Plum off. "He's not friendly. He'll buck anyone who tries to ride him."

Mercedes trudged out of the main building just then.

Her clothing and curly hair were dusty, and her cheek was badly scraped.

"She tried to ride him," Taylor said, seizing on a desperate plan.

"Is that true?" Beverly asked Mercedes.

"No," Mercedes replied.

"Yes, it is!" Taylor insisted firmly, hoping to convey something in her voice that would tip Mercedes to go along with the deceit.

"No," Mercedes maintained.

"Then how did . . . that . . . happen to you?" Beverly questioned.

"I was only trying to get a halter on. I wasn't even thinking of riding. I'm not that crazy."

Taylor chewed her bottom lip nervously, not daring to even breathe or do anything to change this good luck. Mercedes had completely misunderstood which horse they were talking about.

"What about that horse?" Beverly asked, nodding at Shafir.

"She's a wonderful horse!" Taylor said, speaking before Mercedes would have a chance to say anything to the contrary. "We just got her from Ross River Ranch."

"Ross River Ranch," Beverly echoed, and from her tone it was clear she was impressed.

Mercedes shot Taylor a puzzled look.

Taylor answered her with a pleading expression. *Just go along with what I'm saying. Please! Please!*

Plum watched Daphne guide Shafir around the ring. The playful young mare seemed to think it was a game and had taken on a prancing gait, her head held high.

"She is pretty," Beverly commented.

"Beautiful," Taylor agreed. "This horse I'm on is at least fifteen, maybe older. That horse, Shafir, is only five. She's a little behind on her training, but she's very smart and cooperative." Taylor glanced quickly at Mercedes. *Don't say she's not cooperative*, Taylor's eyes implored.

Mercedes gave a light, fast wink, and Taylor relaxed a little. She had figured out what Taylor was up to and wasn't going to say anything.

Mrs. LeFleur came out of the main building, an inquisitive look on her face.

"Mrs. LeFleur," Beverly greeted her.

"Oh, hi, Mrs. L., you're here after all!" Taylor greeted her with a nervous laugh. "What do you know? I didn't see you."

"What are you talking about?" Mrs. LeFleur asked.

Ignoring the question, Taylor gestured toward Plum and her mother. "Good thing you're here now. The Masons are interested in leasing Shafir."

Taylor wished Mrs. LeFleur didn't wear such thick glasses. Not being able to see her eyes made it hard to read her expression. Time seemed to crawl as Mrs. LeFleur stood there without saying anything.

"Mrs. Mason, come to my office and let's discuss it," Mrs. LeFleur said finally.

Taylor dismounted. By the time she came around in front of Prince Albert, Mercedes had gone into the corral with Daphne.

"You know," Plum said before Taylor could escape into the stable, "you're not a better rider than me."

"I never said I was," Taylor replied.

"Yeah, but you think it."

"How do you know what I think?"

"Puh-lease. It's easy enough to tell. You think I couldn't ride any horse that you could ride? Not likely."

"Not any horse, just Prince Albert."

"That's because you let him do whatever he wants. You're a pushover and he knows it."

"Plum, you don't usually talk to me, do you?"

"No. You're right. I usually don't talk to you."

"Well, keep up the good work," Taylor said as she took hold of Prince Albert's halter and steered him toward the main building.

Chapter 18

I feel so guilty," Taylor told Daphne late that afternoon. Along with Mercedes, they had just finished mucking and haying all four stalls. They had groomed, watered, and fed the horses. Mercedes's mother had come for her, honking the horn impatiently until she ran out to the car. Daphne was waiting for her father, and Taylor was keeping her company on the picnic table outside the corral under the towering maple.

"Why, because you lied to the Masons?" Daphne asked as she ran a brush through her long, silky hair.

"I didn't exactly lie. Besides, I don't feel bad about that. I feel terrible about what I've done to Shafir."

"Hmmm," Daphne mused, a serious expression on her face. "That."

"Yeah. That," Taylor echoed miserably. "I started talking without thinking — which is something I do way too much, I know. But I was so scared that she was going take out a lease on Prince Albert. I don't think he could take the abuse Plum dishes out. It could kill him!"

"At least that didn't happen," Daphne said. Plum and her mother had become fascinated by Shafir's elegant beauty. Suddenly, Prince Albert was no longer interesting to them. They'd driven away happy with a signed lease for Shafir.

Mrs. LeFleur had also said she was pleased. The Masons would now be paying for part of Shafir's upkeep. It made the young horse less of a drain on Wildwood's slim financial resources.

But Taylor now felt awful. What terrible fate had she brought down on lovely, playful Shafir?

"We'll watch her," Daphne said after they'd sat together a while longer in glum silence.

"What do you mean?" Taylor asked.

"Every time Plum is here, one of us has to stay with

her. That way we can stop her from doing anything too awful."

"Good plan, but Plum can't stand me. She thinks I'm beneath her. She won't want me hanging around," Taylor pointed out.

"Then you have to change that. Mercedes and I have other things to do. We can't be with her every second. Besides, if you don't mind me saying it, you're the one who talked her into the lease."

"I know!" Taylor cried unhappily. "But we've never liked each other — not since first grade."

"It's no big deal. Just stop treating her like she's got fangs and claws."

"I don't do that!" Taylor objected.

Daphne looked at her and nodded. "Sorry, but you kind of do."

"She does have fangs and claws," Taylor muttered.

"See!"

"Okay! Okay!" Taylor said, laughing lightly despite her gloomy mood. "I'll try."

Daphne's father's car turned into the ranch, and Daphne hopped off the table. "You'll have to do better than try. You've got to convince Plum that you like her," she said as she pulled open the passenger side door.

"I don't know if I can do it," Taylor objected.

"You did a pretty good job of lying your head off today," Daphne teased. "I have faith in you."

"Gee, thanks loads," Taylor said quietly, waving as Daphne and her father drove off.

Mrs. LeFleur came out of the main building and was headed for her green car when she noticed Taylor. "Want a lift home, kiddo?" she offered. "We can toss your bike in the trunk."

"Thanks," Taylor said, taking her bike from the tree where it had been leaning and wheeling it toward the car.

"It's been quite a day, hasn't it?" Mrs. LeFleur remarked as she slammed the trunk shut. "Are you happier now that Prince Albert is safe?"

"Yes, but now I'm worried about Shafir," Taylor admitted.

"You're a big-hearted girl, but you can't worry about everybody," Mrs. LeFleur commented as they both slid into the front seat. "Those slim shoulders won't be able to take the weight after a while."

"But I brought Shafir here. And I'm the one who convinced Plum to lease her."

Mrs. LeFleur started her engine and pulled the car out. "That's true, but Shafir is young and strong. And willful! Plum will have a tough time if she tries to dominate her by force. I'll keep an eye on Plum, too."

"Do you know about what she should be doing?" Taylor asked. "Will you be able to tell if she's doing something bad?" She was never sure how much Mrs. LeFleur actually knew about horses.

"I may not have ridden in thirty years, but I rode a great deal before that. Someday I'll tell you about it, but not now. I am weary from the day's activities. Trust me, though. I know what's good for a horse."

Mrs. LeFleur's reassuring words flooded Taylor with relief. "Thank you. Thank you for everything," she said with heartfelt gratitude.

"Dear girl, no need to thank me," Mrs. LeFleur replied. "No need at all."

Chapter 19

When Taylor walked in the door, her mother was in the living room speaking spiritedly to someone on her cell phone. "Absolutely! Not a problem. I'll be over tomorrow and we can plan your menu. My pleasure! See you tomorrow." Jennifer turned and smiled when she noticed Taylor. "I have been on the phone all day with people who were at the luncheon yesterday. I've booked four dinners, a luncheon, and a church social. Plus, I'm going to meet with two possible jobs tomorrow." Jennifer pulled Taylor into a tight hug. "We did it, Taylor! We were a hit!"

"You did it, Mom. Claire and I just helped."

"I couldn't have done it without your help," Jennifer

insisted. Breaking from the hug, Jennifer studied Taylor. "Sit down a minute. I want to talk to you."

Taylor sat on the couch and Jennifer sat beside her. "Listen, Taylor, I want you to know that I realize these last months haven't been easy on you. I'm sure you miss Dad, and I've been so absorbed in starting my catering company that I haven't been around for you as much as I used to be. I'm sorry about that. But if this business is successful it will mean so much for both of us. You'll be able to —"

Taylor reached out and touched her mother's arm. "I understand," she said. "I really do. What you're doing takes a lot of your time. But you're doing it to make things good for us. I know."

"And you don't mind?"

"Sometimes I mind," she admitted. "But I can deal."

Jennifer reached over and hugged Taylor once more. "You're the best," she said.

"You're the best, too," Taylor replied.

After a moment, Taylor got up. "I'd better do my homework."

"It's Sunday night, and you still haven't done your homework?" Jennifer asked pointedly.

"I'm doing it now."

Taylor headed for the stairs to go to her room. "By the way," Jennifer said, "Travis called."

A flutter of happiness flew through Taylor. "What did he want?"

"He said to call him."

The moment Taylor was in her room, she took her cell phone from her pocket: LOW BATTERY. That explained why Travis had called on the home phone. She tried calling him back but the phone died completely.

Taylor went back downstairs and got the cordless house phone.

"Homework!" Jennifer reminded her, calling from the kitchen.

"In a minute; my phone died and I want to call Travis." Taylor tried but got the message machine. "It's Taylor. I'm calling you back. Call me."

Upstairs in her room, Taylor opened the laptop computer she and her mother shared. She knew she should get to the report that she owed Mr. Romano, but she couldn't resist a quick Internet search first. Typing in the name Bernice LeFleur, Taylor waited while the hard drive searched.

Taylor clicked on the first of five websites, which was

an old edition of the *New York Times*. It was a society page from 1968. There was a picture of an elegant woman with long, straight black hair in a white minidress with a wreath of white flowers around her forehead. Beside her was a handsome man in a tuxedo. He had shoulder-length blond hair. The subhead was: SOCIALITE DEVON MOORE TO WED TYCOON'S SON, HARRISON ROSS.

Taylor wrinkled her nose in confusion. She'd searched for Mrs. LeFleur, not Mrs. Ross.

Then she saw it.

Behind the young Mrs. Ross was an even younger-looking woman. She had long, straight hair parted in the middle and wide, expressive, heavily lined eyes. Scanning the article, Taylor discovered that someone named Bernice LeFleur had been the matron of honor.

Mrs. Ross and Mrs. LeFleur did know each other!

And they'd been close, too.

Now Taylor was dying to know what had happened between them.

At school the next day, Travis was not on the bus nor was he at school. Taylor was dying to call him — he hadn't called her back, and she wanted to know why he'd called in the first place — but cell phones were forbidden at school.

Taylor saw Plum in the hall. She was surrounded by her usual crowd of friends.

Taking a deep breath to get up her nerve, Taylor forced herself to call out to Plum. She was determined to do as Daphne had suggested and make Plum think she liked her. "Hi, Plum," she said brightly. "You got a great horse. It was fun yesterday, wasn't it?"

Plum glared at her in disbelief. "I don't talk to you, remember?"

"Oh, did you take that seriously? I was just joking!"

"Yeah, whatever," Plum grumbled, without stopping. Feeling completely stupid, Taylor watched Plum shrug her shoulders as she moved down the hall and her friends asked what *that* had been about.

"See ya at the ranch!" Taylor called after her.

When Plum turned the corner of the hall, Taylor pressed her forehead into her locker, feeling like a total idiot. How mortifying!

"Are you feeling well, Taylor?" Mr. Romano asked, an expression of bewilderment and concern etched on his face. It was obvious that he'd witnessed her encounter with Plum. "Should I be sending you to the nurse?"

"Probably," Taylor replied drolly.

That afternoon, Taylor stopped her bike under the Wildwood Lane sign and punched in the numbers to Travis's cell phone. It was the sixth time she'd called him, and this time she got the same response as before: "Travis Ryan is not available. To leave a message, press one. . . ." For the fifth time, Taylor clicked off. She didn't want to leave another message. She needed to speak to her best friend.

He *was* her best friend, after all. Taylor knew friends could drift apart, but she wasn't going to let that just happen — not if she could help it, though she wasn't sure if she could.

Taylor wanted to tell him what she'd been thinking and feeling: Balancing everything in her life wasn't easy, and maybe she wasn't doing a very good job of it, either. Being suddenly responsible for Pixie and Prince Albert was a huge job. When she'd taken it on, she'd had no idea how hard it would be. Her life had changed because of it, but she didn't want their friendship to change. She would try hard to make time for him if he would try to understand how much being here at Wildwood Stables meant to her.

Taylor continued on down Wildwood Lane. When she got to the ranch's entrance, she braked and took in a short, sharp gasp of air.

Mrs. LeFleur had replaced the old, peeling sign!

The new sign had a blue field and a green border. The writing was in black, outlined with gold. In elegant, swirling calligraphy, it read:

WILDWOOD STABLES
HOME OF HAPPY HORSES AND PONIES
ALL EQUINE LOVERS WELCOME
Horses Boarded * Riding Lessons * Trail Rides Available

Taylor noticed that her cheeks felt odd, and realized she was smiling. A bubble of happiness rose in her throat and came out as light laughter.

The sign made the ranch so real. Mrs. LeFleur wouldn't have posted it if she didn't believe things were going to go well.

Continuing on into the ranch, Taylor stopped at the big maple, got off, and leaned her bike on it. No one was in the corral, so she went immediately to see how Prince Albert and Pixie were doing. When she got there, she pulled the apples she'd brought out of her pocket. She fed one to each of them.

A shrill neighing came from Mandy's stall, which was next to Pixie's. Mandy bobbed her gray head up and down eagerly. "I brought one for you, don't worry," Taylor told Mandy.

Shafir's head jutted out of the next stall. "And for you, too, wild girl," Taylor added, offering both horses an apple apiece.

Turning back toward Prince Albert, Taylor saw that someone had bolted a steel plate over the splintered top of the stall door where Prince Albert had been cribbing.

Something banged in an empty stall next to Prince Albert's. Taylor was startled when Travis surprised her by popping up from behind the door. "There was a loose board in there. It's all fixed now." He nodded toward the toolbox his father had given him.

"Travis! What are you doing here?"

"I'm in charge of buildings and grounds, remember?"

"Why weren't you in school?"

"I didn't feel like going."

"What do you mean? Your mother let you stay home?" Taylor knew that was unlikely. Travis's mother was on the strict side.

Travis's eyes darted from left to right, checking if anyone else was in listening distance. "I faked being sick," he whispered.

"Why?" Taylor asked softly.

"George Santos. I have to shake him."

"Why?" Taylor asked again.

Travis stepped closer. Once more, he glanced around warily. Then he leaned in close to Taylor. "He wants to be with me every second. He either wants me to come over or is calling me."

"I thought you and he were good friends. Don't you like him?"

"He's a nice guy," Travis said.

"So?"

"He's boring, Taylor. He's so, so boring. I've . . . mmmmm . . . you."

A small smile came to Taylor's face. "Did you mean to say . . . missed? You've missed me?"

Travis sighed, and then he nodded.

Taylor's little grin became a radiant beam of happiness. "I've . . . mmmm . . . you, too." She beckoned for him to follow her down to Shafir's stall.

"Was it you who put the steel plate over Prince Albert's stall?"

"Yeah, that bossy girl told me to."

Taylor didn't even have to ask whom he meant. "Well, thanks."

"You're welcome."

"I've been calling you. Why didn't you call back?" Taylor asked.

"I lost my phone somewhere."

"Oh, good."

"That's not good," Travis said, baffled.

"It's not good that you lost your phone. But I thought you weren't answering my phone calls."

"Oh," Travis replied. "I wouldn't do that."

"Look here," Taylor said, pointing to the lock on the stable door. "This lock sticks. Do you think there's any way you could fix it?"

"Maybe," Travis said, rummaging through his toolbox and pulling out a small can of hinge lubricant.

"Where did this horse come from?" Travis asked.

Taylor told him the story of getting Shafir from Mrs. Ross. "Plum took the lease on her instead of Prince Albert," she added. "But all of us are going to watch over her all the time and make sure she's okay."

"I guess that's what friends do," Travis commented.

"Yeah, friends are good that way," Taylor agreed. All the words about friendship that Taylor had meant to say flew out of her head. "Thanks for coming down here," she said simply. "I've been distracted lately, but I'll do better."

"It's okay," Travis said, keeping his eyes on the excess lubricant he was rubbing off the lock. "I'll do better, too."

Things might not be perfect — maybe nothing was ever perfect — but, to her, they were suddenly looking bright here at Wildwood Stables, the best place in the world.

Come back to

WILDWOOD STABLES

Racing Against Time

Turn the page for a sneak peek!

Taylor and Daphne approached the corral closest to the main building, riding at a jog. Pixie hurried behind, her short legs scurrying to keep up.

Plum Mason and Shafir eyed each other in the middle of the corral. Plum held a lunge line that was looped around Shafir's neck. In her hand was a lunge whip. She stood with the line in her left hand and the whip in her right as she tried to make Shafir walk circles around her.

Plum's slim shoulders were tight, slightly hunched with tension. Shafir's ears were not quite flat, but they were back, and her tail was swishing, sure signs of the horse's annoyance.

Shafir turned and started to walk away. Plum gripped the line, pulling back, but Shafir was determined to go and dragged Plum along. The girl dug her heels into the dirt, kicking up dust until Shafir stopped. Stepping quickly toward the horse, she whacked the mare's withers hard with the lunge whip.

Shafir flinched away from the impact, making Plum lose her balance for a moment.

Daphne reached the corral gate first, dismounted, and hurried inside. "What are you doing?" she asked.

"Excuse me?" Plum replied haughtily.

"What are you doing?" Daphne repeated, this time speaking pointedly, her voice tinged with irritation. "A lunge whip is for guiding a horse, not hitting her!"

Taylor dismounted from Prince Albert. She hitched him to the corral fence and then did the same to Mandy. There was no need to worry about Pixie; wherever Prince Albert was, that's where Pixie would be.

As Taylor let herself into the corral, she saw that Plum and Daphne were embroiled in a heated argument.

"I leased this horse from the ranch, which means I am entitled to come here whenever I want and do whatever I want with her," Plum insisted.

"No, not whatever you want," Daphne shot back. "You know that Shafir needs to be trained."

"Well, that's what I'm doing," Plum replied.

A girl with long black curls who in jeans and a green hoodie strode purposefully out of the main building toward the corral. "What's the trouble here?" Mercedes Gonzalez asked in her usual take-charge manner.

"You said I could take Shafir, didn't you?" Plum said.

"Yeah. You leased her, right?" Mercedes replied.

"But Shafir isn't ready to ride," Taylor reminded Mercedes.

Mercedes shrugged and then gestured toward Plum. "She holds a lease."

"That entitles her to ride, not to train," Daphne argued.

"I don't know," Mercedes said. "Does it?"

The three girls looked at one another uncertainly. A lease gave Plum the right to ride Shafir whenever she wanted, but could she also train her? That was something Taylor, Daphne, and Mercedes had assumed they would be doing.

"No, I don't think it does," Daphne insisted. "Shafir is still the property of Wildwood Stables."

"We'll just talk to the owner — Mrs. What's-her-name, Flowers or whatever," Plum replied forcefully.

Shafir used this interruption as an opportunity to amble toward Prince Albert, Mandy, and Pixie, who stood on the other side of the fence.

Shafir scooped up a bare stick that had fallen from the spreading maple that grew beside the corral. She pranced with the stick in her mouth, bobbing her head up and down, as if she were the leader of a parade.

"What's she doing?" Plum demanded.

"She's playing," Mercedes informed her. "Arabians are known for it."

Taylor spied a bridle draped over the corral fence. A chain shank was fitted over the nosepiece and dangled from the bottom. "Were you planning to use that on Shafir?"

Plum didn't answer. She kept her focus on Daphne and Mercedes as though Taylor wasn't even there.

"Are you using the chain shank on Shafir?" Taylor asked again.

"Does anyone else hear mosquitoes buzzing?" Plum asked.

Taylor's face reddened with anger. But then she remembered her new plan when dealing with Plum: Stop treating her like she's got fangs and claws. It was the only way she'd get close enough to Plum to make sure she was treating Shafir right.

Taylor felt responsible for Shafir. It was Taylor who'd persuaded Plum that Shafir was a great horse for her to lease. She'd acted out of sheer desperation because Plum was about to lease Prince Albert.

Taylor would not let that happen to Prince Albert. It was a matter of life-and-death.

You belong at
WILDWOOD STABLES

Friendship, rivalry, and the amazing place that
brings them together . . . Read them all!

#1: Daring to Dream

#2: Playing for Keeps

#3: Racing Against Time

#4: Learning to Fly